GATHERING STORMS

Johnnie Alexander

Annie's®

AnniesFiction.com

Books in the Sweet Intrigue series

. . . and more to come!

Library of Congress-in-Publication Data
Gathering Storms / by Johnnie Alexander
p. cm.
I. Title
                    2021934854

AnniesFiction.com
(800) 282-6643
Annie's Sweet Intrigue™
Series Creator: Shari Lohner
Editor: Lorie Jones

10 11 12 13 14 | Printed in South Korea | 9 8 7 6 5 4 3 2 1

Isabelle Byrnes removed an ebony jewelry case from the wall safe that was hidden behind a tropical landscape painted by Livingston Roberts, one of the famed Florida Highwaymen artists, in the 1950s. Isabelle's father, Judge Davis Byrnes, had greatly admired the colorful scene. So did she. Even more so now that her father was gone.

Isabelle opened the lid of the jewelry case to reveal the pearl necklace and matching earrings to her attorney, Reuben Hart, and her stepmother, Heather, who sat on the other side of Dad's immense mahogany desk. "These were a gift to my mother from her parents. To celebrate her sweet sixteen."

Reuben, who had been the family's attorney for more than fifteen years, took the case from Isabelle. "A fine set. Whenever Mathilde wore them to an event we attended, my wife always commented on their quality and called them sophisticated."

"Mother wore them often." Which was why Isabelle seldom did. Her grief, though dulled by time, grew sharp as memories of her mother washed over her. The pain even cut through the larger, fresher grief pressing against Isabelle's heart.

"Your grandparents were very generous to their daughter." Heather waved her ringed fingers at the cases Isabelle had already placed on the desk. "Pearls at sixteen, sapphires at eighteen, emeralds as a wedding gift. So many expensive jewels. That diamond bracelet is to die for." She grimaced and covered her mouth with her lacquered fingertips. "Poor choice of words, I suppose."

Isabelle glanced at Reuben, silently begging him not to respond to her stepmother's thoughtless comment. Though Reuben seldom said anything negative about Heather, Isabelle sensed his growing frustration with Heather's insensitivity to Isabelle's pain. She feared the day that frustration boiled over.

Reuben pressed his lips together, then scanned the document on his electronic tablet. "That's everything on my list. As I said before, the appraisal of your jewels and your father's things—his watches and cuff links—will take place at my office at the end of the week. After that, I'll update the insurance policy."

"Thank you," Isabelle said. "I appreciate how many of these details you handle for me."

"Don't you mean 'for us'?" Petulance marred the lightness of Heather's question.

A petulance Isabelle felt compelled to overlook. "For us," she repeated, forcing a bright smile.

"After all," Heather continued as she eyed the open safe, "you're not the sole heir."

"These jewels were bequeathed to Isabelle in her mother's will," Reuben said evenly. "They have nothing to do with Davis's will or his estate. As I explained before, this appraisal is a routine annual update." A routine appraisal Heather had never been invited to participate in before.

Isabelle rested her hand against the cool metal of the safe door as if seeking support. The day after her father's funeral, Reuben had met with Isabelle and Heather in this very room to discuss the last will and testament—a document with no surprises. When her father remarried, he'd updated his will to include a specific percentage of the estate for his new wife. Both Isabelle and Heather had been present for the signing. At the time, Heather said she understood that Isabelle would inherit the bulk of the estate, and she expressed her appreciation for her husband's generosity.

Isabelle's father had also provided a more than comfortable allowance to his wife while he was alive, but he never complained—at least not to Isabelle—when Heather exceeded it. And she often did.

In the weeks since his death, Heather had grown increasingly combative. She seemed emotionally unbalanced by a strange combination of genuine grief from the untimely loss of her husband and jealousy that he hadn't left her a greater percentage. She frequently complained about being a guest in her own home, despite Isabelle's constant reassurances that wasn't true. Each woman had her own apartment in separate wings of the sprawling mansion. Nothing about their living arrangements needed to change.

"What else is in that secret safe?" Heather asked. "It's like a never-ending well of treasure."

Isabelle blinked back tears, refusing to let Heather see how the flippant remark affected her. She retrieved a cashbox and a thin binder from the safe. "Dad always kept money on hand in case of emergencies." She placed both items on the desk. "The binder holds the family's important documents, such as birth certificates, social security cards, and passports."

Death certificates too, though Isabelle would choke if she tried to say those words. One for her mother and, as soon as she could bring herself to slip it into a sheet protector, one for her father.

"What about deeds?" Heather asked. "Anything like that in the binder?"

"For the estate, yes," Isabelle replied. "And the titles to the vehicles."

"The title to my car?" Heather reached for the binder.

Reuben obtained possession of it first. "Do you want your title? You are certainly at liberty to maintain your own files." He handed the binder to Isabelle.

She flipped to the tab for automobiles, pulled the title to Heather's Audi from its protective sleeve, and slid it across the desk.

Heather stared at it but didn't touch it. "What about that box? How much cash is in there?"

"The box belongs to Isabelle," Reuben said. "Therefore, its contents matter to her alone."

"Davis was my husband." Heather's voice verged on a whine. "I don't understand how you can speak to me as if I meant nothing to him."

"I haven't counted the money." Isabelle knew the cashbox existed. She'd been with her dad on a few occasions when he'd opened it. But the safe itself had been off-limits—an unspoken rule she'd never questioned. When she wanted to wear her mother's pearls or emeralds, Dad retrieved them from the safe for her. Today was the first day she'd punched in the safe's combination. "There may be a few twenties. Perhaps more." She handed the box to Heather. "Take it."

"Don't give me that attitude," Heather said. "It's not like I'm destitute and need your charity. We should have gone through the safe ourselves. Just you and me. We don't need Reuben involved in our private business."

Or you could have let Reuben and me take care of business that doesn't concern you. Isabelle had scheduled the attorney's visit during Heather's weekly spa morning, but Reuben had arrived before Heather left. When she'd learned why he'd come, she went into full victim mode.

"Why didn't you tell me?" she'd demanded. "You know I want to be here for you during these trying times. Give me a minute to reschedule my appointment."

Heather smiled at Isabelle. "You're a considerate person. I know you only want the best for me." She hefted the cashbox and flashed a triumphant smile at Reuben. "It feels heavy."

"I think that's everything." Isabelle ran her fingers along the base of the safe. To her surprise, her fingertips brushed against stiff cardboard. She drew out a black box the size of a document, probably no more than a quarter inch deep, and held it up. "Except for this."

Heather leaned forward, eyes sparkling. "More jewels?"

Before Isabelle could answer, Reuben cleared his throat. "Perhaps you should open that in private."

"Don't be ridiculous," Heather said. "Izzy and I don't have any secrets."

Isabelle held the box close to her chest to center her thoughts. Heather's assertion was ridiculous. True, the woman was near enough in age to Isabelle—a mere eight years older—that she considered her more of a friend than a mother. But they weren't best friends, and Isabelle rarely confided in Heather. Since her mother's death a few weeks before Isabelle's ninth birthday, her confidant had been her father.

As a child, Isabelle had spent part of each day in this sanctuary of books, family portraits, and valuable heirlooms. During the school year, she finished her homework at a small desk by the window. In more recent years, she joined her father here in the evening lull before dinner, and they talked about their day. About everything. About nothing.

Yet she'd never seen this box before.

How long had it been hidden at the back of the safe, unseen and unacknowledged? Perhaps even forgotten?

"Come on," Heather urged, her gaze glued to the box. "Open it already."

The childish impulse to remind her stepmother that she couldn't tell her what to do flitted through Isabelle's mind. Maybe she'd finally had enough of Heather's insistence on making decisions that weren't hers to make, her gradual taking over of the household staff, and her sudden interest in estate affairs that she'd ignored during her marriage.

Even if Isabelle waited to open the box, Heather's meddling curiosity wouldn't end. If she opened the box now, Reuben could provide any needed support. She opened one end and peeked inside to find two embossed certificates. Birth certificates.

How strange. All the family documents, dating back to their historical roots in seventeenth-century England, were carefully cataloged in archival sleeves. The exceptions were the current documents kept in the safe. What possible reason could Dad have had for stashing any of the family birth certificates in the dark recesses of the safe?

As Isabelle scanned both documents, her stomach clenched at the birth date on the second. *Her* birth date.

She read the document more slowly. Baby Girl Blacke had been born in December in Volusia County in Florida. Her mother's name was Michelle Blacke. There was no father listed.

Isabelle switched to the other certificate. The birth date was listed three years before hers in December. Baby Boy Blacke had been born in Miami-Dade County in Florida to Michelle Blacke. Again, there was no father listed.

She recalled all the family surnames, but she couldn't remember a Blacke in any of the records she'd studied. Or even a Michelle. As often as she'd scrutinized the family tree, she would definitely recognize the name if it was anywhere in the family documents.

So who were these children?

Was *she* one of these children?

No. After all, Isabelle shared her dad's hair color—at least until his hair had turned silver. They even shared the same single dimple in their left cheek.

A million thoughts raced through her mind, but one stood out. Perhaps Michelle Blacke was her true mother. But then why wasn't Davis listed as the baby's father?

And what about the boy? If Isabelle was Michelle Blacke's daughter, then Baby Boy Blacke would be her brother. At least, her half brother if Davis wasn't his dad too.

Heather rounded the desk and peered over Isabelle's shoulder at the certificates. "What are those?"

Isabelle handed them to her. "Dad never told you about them?"

"Told me what?" Heather glanced at the certificates. "Who's Michelle Blacke?"

"I don't know," Isabelle answered.

"But this is your birthday." Heather pointed to Baby Girl Blacke's date of birth. "This must be your birth certificate."

Isabelle flipped open the binder to her tab. "Here's mine." The certificate named Isabelle Elizabeth Byrnes as the daughter of Mathilde and Davis Byrnes. Weighing seven pounds and one ounce. The other certificate couldn't be hers.

"Maybe you have a twin."

Ignoring Heather's lame attempt at a joke, Isabelle took the certificates and handed them to Reuben. "What do you know about these?"

He read them both, then shook his head. "Nothing. Davis never mentioned . . . I don't know who these children are."

For the first time Isabelle could remember, Reuben appeared flustered.

"Then these certificates can't mean anything." Heather folded her arms across her chest. "I say we burn them. They can't do either of us any good."

"Absolutely not." Isabelle was almost as shocked by Heather's suggestion as she was by the discovery of the certificates. The thought of destroying legal documents went against both her personal and professional code of ethics. Even if the documents had nothing to do with her, Isabelle could never destroy official certificates. They represented individuals—leaves on a family tree.

Perhaps her family tree.

"Davis must have kept these for a reason," Reuben said. "That the secret died with him may be unfortunate. Or perhaps—and I can't believe I'm saying this—it is for the best."

"Of course it's for the best." Heather flounced back to her seat. "Isn't it obvious what happened here?"

"What do you mean?" Isabelle asked.

"Grow up," Heather told her. "Your father must have been involved with this Michelle Blacke somehow. We don't need any long-lost heirs casting aspersions on his good name. Or trying to lay claim to his estate."

"But what if I'm the baby girl?" Isabelle asked.

"Impossible. That would mean . . ." Heather shifted her gaze to Reuben. "You know what that would mean."

Isabelle bit her lip and looked away. She didn't need Heather or Reuben to spell out what they were both thinking.

Mere minutes before, Isabelle would have agreed there was no way her father could have been involved with another woman while married to her mom. But now? What if her dad did have an affair with Michelle Blacke? It was unlikely, but what else would explain the certificate with Isabelle's birth date on it?

No. She wouldn't believe it. Not about her dad. And not without more proof.

"I'm going to research these," Isabelle announced. Her firm tone seemed to surprise Heather and Reuben. If only they could see how much she was quaking inside. "I'm a trained genealogist. This is what I do."

"It's best to leave the past alone," Reuben advised. "If Davis didn't tell any of us about this, I'm afraid you might not like what you discover."

"Isabelle," Heather practically purred her name, drawing out the syllables. "I don't think—"

"If you'll excuse me, I'd like to get started right away." Isabelle put the lid on the box and carried it to her room. She needed privacy. She needed to think.

Most of all, she needed answers.

What are these, Dad? Why did you hide them from me?

In frustration coated with grief, Isabelle plopped on her window seat and studied the certificates again. When she turned over the one for the boy, she found a telephone number written in her father's distinctive handwriting across the top corner. It was the same area code the Byrnes would have if their estate were located ten miles farther north. The number could be for Jacksonville or Saint Augustine or anywhere between here and the Georgia state line.

There was an easy way to find out.

The receptionist who answered Isabelle's call told her the business, an independent insurance company located in the barrier island town of Delfin Isle, had celebrated their twenty-fifth anniversary earlier in the year. This was their original phone number, and the woman didn't have any idea who'd had the number before them.

A dead end.

So was Isabelle's online search for Michelle Blacke. The name was too common, even with its unusual spelling, for Isabelle to discover the mother of the two unnamed children.

Tracking the phone number was her one lead. She searched the online directory for Delfin Isle and found the listing for a private investigator named Jasper Long. Her call went to voice mail, and she hung up without leaving a message.

This mystery was too important to hand off to someone else. Instead, Isabelle decided to meet Mr. Long in person. And while she was in Delfin Isle, she'd do her own sleuthing at the local courthouse and newspaper archives.

Despite the tropical storm brewing off the Atlantic coast, Isabelle hurriedly packed for her impromptu trip. Thankfully, Heather was either gone or in her apartment. Isabelle scribbled a brief note explaining where she was going.

After running a few necessary errands in town and filling her gas tank, Isabelle headed north. She drove for about an hour and followed her navigational app across the bridge to the address of the cottage she'd reserved on Delfin Isle. The app directed her through a quaint town square and onto a winding road of wind-bent palms. The charming houses with louvered windows, apparently dating back to the 1940s, were tucked behind overgrown hibiscus bushes and sprawling crape myrtles.

Isabelle maneuvered onto the gravel drive of the last house before the road disappeared into a sandy beach. Beyond the dunes, ocean waves rolled onto the sand, then receded with a roar.

In the presence of such magnificence and power, her confusion and hurt lessened. The tension in her muscles eased, and a strange peace settled within her spirit. She needed answers to her questions about Michelle Blacke and her mystery children. But perhaps Isabelle also needed *this*. A few days away from her stepmother, estate matters, and rooms devoid of her father's comforting laugh.

A place to heal her aching heart.

Isabelle wheeled her suitcase along the cracked sidewalk to the cottage's front stoop. A bouquet of black tulips rested on the welcome mat. *What a pleasant surprise.*

Isabelle cradled the bouquet in one arm, but her knees weakened as she read the card: *Go home . . . or else!*

Jarrod Long, owner of a successful security company, reviewed the three bid requests he'd been handed at the morning briefing—providing security at a new art exhibition gala in Saint Augustine, assessing the security needs of a planned shopping mall on the mainland, and teaming up with law enforcement for the governor's visit next month to their little corner of Florida sunshine.

On paper, the governor's visit appeared the most promising venture, both for monetary considerations and its public relations value. But Jarrod had worked with politicians before. Either they flouted his company's suggestions while still expecting flawless protection, or they considered private security a kind of status symbol worth bragging about. Both viewpoints could endanger his team.

On the other hand, the shopping mall might be a stepping-stone to other large-scale construction projects. Jarrod already had someone in mind to oversee the assessment, a retired army veteran who'd lost a leg in Afghanistan. *If* they won the bid and *if* the developer was suitably impressed, this same veteran could manage a new division catering to similar clients.

Jarrod shifted his attention from the paperwork to the framed photo on his desk. He and his brother, Jasper, stood on the deck of a boat with a huge marlin suspended between them. Jasper had caught the giant fish last summer.

A casual observer may have mistaken the two men in the photo for twins. But Jasper's receding hairline, hidden by the baseball cap he wore, and the deepening lines near his eyes and mouth marked him as the older of the two. That six-year difference hadn't felt like much when they were in their twenties, but now that Jarrod was thirty-two, he saw his future self in his brother.

Except that his brother was happily married and the father of two amazing sons. Meanwhile, Jarrod seemed doomed to bachelorhood. He didn't mind his status as favorite uncle. In fact, he actively encouraged that sentiment with surprise gifts and Jaguars football tickets when he could snag them. As the years slipped by, however, he found it harder to ignore the hole in his heart. An empty place where a wife and children of his own belonged.

He'd thought he met the woman of his dreams in his early twenties. But her career goals had lured her to California while Jarrod's roots were sunk deep into the sandy soil of Delfin Isle. Though time had healed his heartbreak, the chances of finding that special someone at his age felt as likely as discovering buried treasure in his backyard.

Without thinking about it, Jarrod flexed his biceps. The muscles were still there, but not with the definition they'd had during his military days. He definitely needed to spend more time at the gym.

In the end, he signed off on all three bid requests. Even though the art gala wasn't as lucrative as the other two, such events provided needed on-the-job training for his less experienced guards. Winning all three bids was a long shot, but the "casting your bread upon the waters" philosophy of business growth had rewarded him with a flourishing reputation in the security field. The long hours and intense work paid off in both handsome contracts and prominent contacts.

As he finished the last signature, his cell phone rang. "Hey, Jay," he said, referring to Jasper by the nickname they'd given each other. "I hope you're not calling because you're bored on a stakeout. I don't have time for chitchat."

"I wish that's all it was." Jasper's tone was light, but there was an underlying edge in his voice. "How about I buy you a cup of coffee?"

Jarrod glanced at his computer screen. More than twenty unopened messages clamored for his attention along with a pile of paperwork in his in-box. Even in this day and age, not everything was digital. His calendar showed a meeting in thirty minutes and three more that afternoon.

"Could I buy you breakfast in the morning instead?" Jarrod asked. "It's a crazy day."

Jasper didn't immediately answer.

The underlying edge in his brother's voice that Jarrod heard earlier turned into a red alert. His body tensed as he waited for Jasper to respond.

"It's probably nothing," Jasper finally said.

"If it was nothing, you wouldn't have called. What's the matter?"

"Not on the phone."

Even though Jasper couldn't see him, Jarrod nodded. His brother, a private investigator, sometimes came off as excessively security conscious. Or paranoid.

Still, that old saying was sometimes true. *Just because you're paranoid doesn't mean they aren't after you.* But who would be after Jasper?

Silly question. It could be a disgruntled client. A spouse who'd been caught cheating. Jasper often dealt with society's more troubled elements, and he'd been in a few scrapes during his career. But it had been a while since Jasper had sounded so guarded.

"I can give you about ten minutes," Jarrod offered. "Want to meet at Zapped?" The out-of-the-way coffee shop catered to the local crowd and was conveniently located halfway between their respective offices.

"See you there." The call abruptly ended.

When Jarrod arrived at Zapped, Jasper sat hunched at a corner table where he could see the door and the front windows. The very seat Jarrod would have taken if he'd arrived first. Jarrod hurried over to his brother.

Jasper raised a large cup. "Hope you're still drinking that Colombian blend. Fixed it up the way you like it."

"You must want a huge favor." Jarrod took an adjacent chair, giving him a view out the side windows and the hallway leading to the restrooms and a storage area. Between the two of them, they had the coffee shop covered. As if anything nefarious ever happened in this place beyond voices slightly raised in either disagreement or excitement. *Old habits die hard.*

"Not a favor." Jasper frowned as he played with his own cup, tilting it slightly forward. "But I need your ears. And maybe your eyes."

"You've got them."

Jasper leaned closer and lowered his voice. "I got a new client a couple of days ago. Easy money. She had this phone number that belongs to the insurance company on Camellia Drive."

"I know it." The agency had been around as long as Jarrod could remember. "What does she want you to do with it?"

"She wants to find out who had the number before that."

Jarrod sat back in surprise. Why in the world would Jasper go all cloak-and-dagger over an ancient phone number? There had to be more to the story, but he'd need to let Jasper tell it in his own way. "That can't be too hard for an old pro like you."

"Nope." Jasper took a long sip of his drink, then focused on the lid. "I made a few calls, found out the phone company wouldn't help because of privacy concerns. But they have old reverse directories in their archives."

"No surprise."

"Only thing is, while I was driving to the mainland, I got a text from an A. Nonymous."

Jarrod harrumphed at the tired joke. "What did Mr. Nonymous want? Or was it a Ms. Nonymous?"

"Hard to tell. But the message was clear." Jasper pulled his phone from a pocket, tapped on the screen, and slid it toward Jarrod.

The text read: *Stay away from I. B. Or else U B sorry.*

"I take it I. B. is your client?" Jarrod asked, though he knew the answer to his question. And to his next one. "Did it trace back to a burner phone?"

"What do you think?" Jasper shrugged. "Thing is, when my client arrived here at the island, she found a note telling her, and I quote, *'Go home . . . or else!'*"

"All these threats because of an old phone number?" Jarrod shook his head. "Seems a little melodramatic."

"That's what I thought."

"So what is this really about?"

Jasper hesitated.

Both brothers walked a fine line at times when it came to client confidentiality. Even when they needed the other one's input or advice, they were careful to keep the flow of information to a minimum without a client's explicit permission.

"Birth certificates." Jasper raised his hands, then let them drop. "Threats like this aren't a big deal in my line of work. They happen. I wouldn't have called you except . . ." He glanced away, but not before Jarrod noted the worry clouding his brother's expression.

Jarrod drank his coffee, giving Jasper the space he needed to compose himself and gather his thoughts. The blend was robust, the bitterness lessened by the raw sugar and splash of cream Jasper had added to the cup.

"Someone broke into my office sometime last night," Jasper announced. The words came out clipped, emotionless.

Jarrod froze. "How did that happen?"

"Several case files were stolen," Jasper continued as if Jarrod hadn't spoken. "Including my newest client's."

Jarrod's stomach dropped. The security system he'd installed had been top-notch five years ago when Jasper moved into his new office on the island. But their planned upgrades never happened—sometimes because of Jarrod's schedule and other times because of Jasper's. "Didn't the alarm go off? What about the cameras?"

"Whoever broke in knew what they were doing," Jasper said. "At least I still have digital backups of the stolen files."

"Did you call the police?"

"I called you. I think someone wanted copies of those birth certificates, but I can't imagine why. They may have taken the other files as a diversion."

"That's possible."

"It's more than the theft." Jasper was clearly crestfallen. "I know I shouldn't be thinking about myself, but I can't help it. Do you know what this will do to my credibility, my professionalism, if anyone finds out? I'll be ruined."

"That's not going to happen," Jarrod assured him.

"I'm supposed to help people." Jasper pounded the table with his fist. "I keep their troubles and their secrets to myself. I need to find the lowlife who did this without involving the police, so can we keep this break-in between the two of us?"

Jarrod nodded. As much as he hated to do it, he checked his watch. "I have a meeting I can't get out of in a few minutes. But I'll come over after that. Don't touch anything."

"I appreciate it." Jasper seemed to relax for the first time since Jarrod had arrived. "I knew I could count on you."

"Yeah, well, I appreciate the coffee." Jarrod picked up his cup, then took another sip.

Jasper started to reply when his phone vibrated. He answered the call, giving monosyllabic responses that made little sense to Jarrod even as his brother became more agitated.

"I've got to go." Jasper stood and pocketed his phone. "Come as soon as you can," he said before hurrying from the coffee shop.

"Wait a minute," Jarrod called after him. "What was that about?"

Jasper turned when he reached the door. "As soon as you can." He exited the coffee shop without waiting for a reply.

Jarrod released a heavy sigh. He had no idea how long it would take to process Jasper's office. Extra hands would make the job go faster, and he trusted a few men on his team with his life. But he also respected his brother's request to keep the break-in between the two of them.

He arrived at his office with a couple of minutes to spare. Though he found his thoughts wandering to Jasper's plight and his mysterious phone call, he managed to keep the agenda moving along.

As the meeting was winding down, his phone vibrated. *Jasper.*

Jarrod excused himself to take the call. "Patience, grasshopper. I'm leaving the office in two minutes."

"Make it quick." Jasper's voice came out in a raspy whisper.

An explosive noise reverberated through the phone, and Jarrod jerked away from the device. Even so, he heard Jasper's groan.

"Jay?" Ignoring the others gathered for the meeting, Jarrod ran out of the room. "Jasper, answer me."

"Are you Jarrod?" a feminine voice asked. Her tone was rushed, almost desperate.

"Who's this?"

"I'm with Jasper." Her voice hitched. "He's been shot."

"Is he alive?" Jarrod asked, his heart thundering in his chest.

The line went dead.

Isabelle dropped the phone as blood poured from the bullet wound in Jasper's chest. She needed to focus on applying pressure. And she needed to call for help.

She didn't know who the private investigator had called. Only a name. *Jarrod.* He'd asked if Jasper was alive in the second before she ended the call and dialed 911.

"What is your emergency?" the operator answered, her voice steady and professional.

At first, Isabelle didn't know how to respond. How could she explain the horror of what had happened? She took a deep breath. "He's been shot. Jasper, I mean. Jasper Long." The words tumbled over each other.

Isabelle answered the operator's other questions, pressing a towel she'd found in the bathroom onto the wound. "I think whoever did this is gone." At least, she hoped so. But as much as she feared for her safety, she couldn't leave Jasper in this condition.

"Stay on the line with me," the operator said. "I've dispatched assistance to your location."

"How do you know my location?"

"From your phone's GPS."

Isabelle continued pressing on the wound. Her vision dimmed, and she thought she might faint. "I can't stop the bleeding," she said, her voice wavering.

"It will be all right," the operator said. "Medical assistance and law enforcement are on their way."

At that welcome news, Isabelle's senses went on high alert. "I think I hear the sirens."

"Stay with me until they get there."

The words were barely out before uniformed officers entered the office, their guns drawn, and scanned the room.

One of them knelt beside Isabelle, quickly assessing the situation and placing his hands on hers. "You can let go," he said quietly. "I've got this."

She merely nodded, as if all her words had been used up in the 911 call.

The other officer, a Hispanic woman, holstered her gun as she approached Isabelle. "Are you hurt, ma'am?"

Isabelle shook her head, and images of the past several minutes sped through her mind. She closed her eyes, but that merely heightened her impressions of the impossible scenario.

"I'm Officer Elena Torres. Can you tell me what happened?"

"We were talking." Isabelle couldn't remember the topic of their conversation. Did it even matter? A routine conversation—at least as routine as any conversation could be between a client and her private investigator.

"Then what happened?" Officer Torres prompted.

A burst of sirens shattered the quiet island atmosphere, then ended abruptly.

Isabelle gazed toward the window. The glass had been broken by an errant bullet.

Within seconds, EMTs crowded into the small office.

Too many people. Too many questions. Isabelle stared at her hands. Too much blood. Her head spun, and the room seemed to swirl around her.

"I've got you," Officer Torres assured her. "You're going to be fine."

"What about Jasper?" Isabelle managed to ask despite the dryness in her mouth. "Will he be fine too?" She glanced to where the fallen detective lay surrounded by EMTs.

"I promise they'll do everything they can for him," Officer Torres said.

Another officer joined them, an older man with an air of authority and a steady, no-nonsense expression. "I'm Captain Jerome Palmer. And you are?"

"Isabelle Byrnes." She glanced around the office. "I have identification here somewhere. In my purse."

"Can you tell me why you're here?" the captain asked.

"It's a personal matter," Isabelle answered. "I hired Mr. Long to find some information for me."

"Must be serious information to lead to this," Palmer remarked.

Isabelle frowned. She didn't want to discuss her personal business with the captain. Besides, how could a phone number have led to Jasper getting shot? Especially a phone number from thirty years ago.

Plus, she'd been raised to honor confidentiality. Her father had often stressed the importance of attorney-client privilege, and Isabelle also respected her own clients' privacy. She'd never divulge anything she discovered about a client's ancestors to anyone except that client. Not even a spouse, sibling, or parent.

Now, in this surreal moment when EMTs tried to stabilize a man she'd been casually talking with just a short while ago, her reticence felt like a necessary defense from a danger she couldn't identify.

It only she could call her dad and ask for his advice.

Tears threatened as renewed grief swept over her.

"Ms. Byrnes?" Captain Palmer's voice was gentle but firm. "Is there anything you can tell me about what happened?"

"The office was like this when I arrived." Isabelle gestured toward the ransacked files. "Jasper had been here a couple of minutes when that door opened." She pointed to a door leading to a small side patio. The patio and grassy area were enclosed by a tall privacy fence. "A woman came in. She had a gun, and she aimed it at me. Jasper saved my life."

Palmer took notes. "What did the woman look like?"

"She wore a ski mask." Isabelle let out a hysterical chuckle. "When I first saw her, I noticed the mask before the gun. It was so ludicrous. A mask like that here in Florida? They're rare even in the winter."

"What about her height and weight?" Captain Palmer asked. "The color of her skin, her hair? Anything?"

Isabelle closed her eyes, trying to recall what had happened when the woman had entered the room. She remembered being startled when the door had burst open. Time seemed to stop as she'd attempted to make sense of what was completely illogical. "She wore all black, even black gloves. I didn't see her hair or skin. But she was probably about my height. Slender. Though I don't think she was very athletic."

"Why would you say that?" Officer Torres asked.

Isabelle struggled to think what had given her that impression, but she couldn't come up with a reason. "I'm sorry. I don't know. But amid the flying bullets and the blood, my brain somehow registered that."

"Do you believe you were the intended target?" Captain Palmer asked. "Not Mr. Long?"

A cold shiver raced down Isabelle's spine. "She pointed the gun at me, so yes."

"But you won't tell me why you're here?" Palmer insisted. "Talking to a PI?"

"I promise you," Isabelle said. "It wasn't anything important enough to get me killed."

"Maybe you should let me be the judge of that."

"I'm sure it's something else. But . . ." Isabelle bit her lip, pondering what she should say. Even if she didn't want to discuss the birth certificates, perhaps she should tell the captain about the black tulips.

Then it hit her—that was what Jasper had been saying when the woman opened the door. He'd been encouraging Isabelle to file a police report about the flowers and the note she'd found on her arrival at the beach cottage. He'd started to tell her something that must have been important when they'd been interrupted.

"I rented a cottage on the ocean side of the island," Isabelle said. "When I arrived, I found a bouquet of black tulips and a note telling me to go home."

"Any idea who wrote that note?" Captain Palmer asked.

"None."

The door opened, and a man entered. He quickly took in the scene, pausing as his gaze met Isabelle's. "What happened here?" he asked no one in particular as he rushed to Jasper's side.

The man closely resembled Jasper. Isabelle recalled the name displayed on Jasper's phone. Was this Jarrod, the man Jasper had called, the one she had talked to? A family member?

Her face flushed with anxiety and embarrassment. Isabelle had told him that Jasper had been shot, then hung up. What a cruel thing to do. But in the moment, her thoughts had been consumed with getting help and doing what she could for Jasper.

Captain Palmer touched Isabelle's shoulder. "Why don't you go with Officer Torres and get cleaned up? But don't leave. I have a few more questions."

Isabelle nodded and climbed to her feet. Her legs wobbled, and it took all her strength to stand on her own.

Officer Torres guided Isabelle to a restroom. The officer got the water running and pulled a few paper towels from the dispenser. "That'll get you started," she said before leaving Isabelle alone.

Isabelle studied herself in the mirror, barely recognizing the person staring back at her. The curls she'd carefully created with her hot iron earlier in the day hung like tired strands of seaweed. Mascara dotted the skin beneath her eyes.

She stuck her hands beneath the flow of warm water, grateful to Officer Torres for this small kindness. Not wanting to see the blood on her hands, she lifted her head and gulped in air.

When the heat of the water became too much, Isabelle pushed soap from the dispenser and scrubbed her hands, wrists, and lower arms. The running water was clear as it flowed onto her hands and crimson as it pooled near the drain.

The heat of the water reddened her skin as she washed her hands. As if she could ever cleanse them enough to be rid of the awful memory.

A knock sounded at the door. "Are you okay?" Officer Torres asked.

"Coming," Isabelle said, her voice husky. She cleared her throat and tried again. "Be right out."

By the time she entered the main office, Jasper and most of the EMTs were gone. The man who resembled Jasper, who'd raced in and gone to Jasper's side, stood near the doorway with Captain Palmer and a couple of paramedics.

The captain approached her. "You've been through quite an ordeal. The paramedics will drive you to the hospital. I'll be around later to take your statement and ask a few more questions."

Isabelle nodded, then accompanied the paramedics to a waiting ambulance. One EMT helped her to a sitting position on a gurney while another spread a thin blanket over her. Despite the warmth of Florida's autumn sun, the blanket felt comforting. It was a poor substitute for a father's hug, but it was still a welcome touch.

The first paramedic wrapped her upper arm in a blood pressure cuff with deft movements. He listened to her chest and her heart and recorded her vitals on a chart.

The man who resembled Jasper came out the door. He scanned the area, then strode toward Isabelle. "You were the woman on the call." It wasn't a question.

"I'm sorry I hung up on you. I had to call 911."

"Who shot my brother?"

His directness confirmed that she'd been right—this man was definitely related to Jasper. "I wish I knew. I'm sorry for what happened. Will he be okay?"

"We don't know."

For the first time since the shooting, a wave of guilt washed over her. Even when she'd told Captain Palmer that Jasper had protected her, she hadn't processed the significance of his sacrifice. But as she faced his brother, her cheeks burned. If Jasper died, his blood would be on her hands. She pulled at her fingers as if trying in vain to scrub nonexistent blood from her skin.

His blood on her hands. Both literally and figuratively.

"Tell me what happened," the man said. "Please."

"Jasper protected me." One part of Isabelle's brain noted the gold flecks in his hazel irises while the other considered and discarded a multitude of sentences that sounded too trite, too imperfect for a situation like this. Finally, she shrugged, though the casual gesture was at odds with the depth of her feelings. "He saved my life. I'm sorry."

The man held her gaze a moment longer before shifting his focus to the small crowd across the street. The onlookers were prevented from coming closer by a line of yellow tape that had been stretched between several trees.

"It's what he would do," the man said. "Never one to back down from danger."

The paramedic removed the blood pressure cuff. "We're going to take you to the hospital. Just as a precaution. You've had a shock, and your body needs time to recover. I'd like to go ahead and start an IV, if you don't have any objections."

"Is that really necessary?" Isabelle rubbed her arm where the cuff had been. "I feel fine." That was a lie. She felt shaky and on the verge of a total meltdown, but that didn't mean she needed to go to the hospital.

"I highly recommend it," the paramedic answered. "Better safe than sorry."

"I agree," the man said. He forced a smile and held out his hand. "By the way, I'm Jarrod Long."

She shook his hand. "Isabelle Byrnes."

"I. B." Jarrod gave her a long, lingering look. "Did Jasper tell you about the anonymous text he received?"

What was Jarrod talking about? "No."

"Seems someone told him to stay away from I. B. Or else."

Isabelle's stomach knotted. "From me?" Why hadn't Jasper told her about the text?

"Someone broke into his office and stole a few files. Including yours."

"Jasper told me that. But I don't know why anyone would."

Jarrod placed his hands on the edge of the gurney and leaned close to Isabelle. The golden flecks in his eyes darkened to a rich amber. "I don't have a private investigator's license, but my business is security. You can trust me as much as you trust Jasper."

Isabelle wasn't so sure about that.

Jarrod glanced at the paramedics, who had stepped far enough away to give them privacy but stayed close enough to monitor Isabelle. "Why did you hire my brother?" he whispered in the narrow space between them.

"I asked him to track down a phone number."

"That's it?" His harsh manner suggested that she was lying. He might as well have accused her outright.

From deep inside, a small ember of anger rose within her. How dare he take that tone with her? Of course, he was concerned for Jasper, but Isabelle had been the intended victim. What if this woman in a ski mask tried again?

That thought, rising for the first time, transformed her anger into an abyss of fear. After she'd told Jasper about the birth certificates, he'd been threatened and shot. What if she told Jarrod about them and something happened to him? She was responsible for Jasper's injuries. How could she live with herself if the mysterious woman shot someone else?

"I'm a patient man, but my fuse is getting short," Jarrod said. "I'm going to ask you again. Why did you hire my brother?"

"I told you why." Isabelle somehow managed to make her voice sound firmer than she would have thought possible under the circumstances. She could at least tell him what she already told Captain Palmer. After all, he'd probably ask the captain for a copy of the police report.

"I got a threatening message too," she finally said. "It was on the porch of the cottage I rented."

"Jasper told me about the note."

"So you also know about the black tulips."

Jarrod raised his eyebrows. "Tulips? He didn't mention tulips to me—not black or red or any other color."

"The note was with a bouquet of black tulips. They were on the porch."

"Is there some significance to black tulips?"

"Depends on who you ask." Isabelle paused. She had done an online search on the language of flowers once she'd locked herself inside the cottage that first night. "Some websites say they symbolize power or strength. But they aren't truly black. They have a faint purple hue that can symbolize royalty."

"What else?"

She held his gaze. "They can represent what black usually represents."

The two of them simultaneously breathed a single word. "Death."

Jarrod stared after the ambulance as it drove away with Isabelle Byrnes tucked safely inside. Despite the unsettling circumstances of their meeting, he'd been struck by her poise and calm demeanor. She was understandably shaken, but she hadn't swooned or fallen apart. Instead, she'd managed to administer first aid to Jasper and answer Jarrod's questions.

To be more accurate, she'd answered the questions she chose to answer.

But poise under pressure didn't mean Isabelle wasn't mistaken about the shooter's intent. In the heat of the moment, she may have believed herself to be the intended victim when Jasper was the true target. Frightened witnesses often mixed up details. Jarrod knew from his own experiences that even seasoned warriors suffered from fear when bullets started flying. But they were trained to control that fear and be aware of their surroundings no matter the circumstances. He sincerely doubted Isabelle in her tailored dress and designer heels could do the same when overwhelming emotions surged through her.

When Jarrod and his brother had talked at the coffee shop, Jasper had seemed certain the office break-in was tied to the anonymous text he'd received. He'd also been concerned about the threatening note Isabelle had found at her rental. But why hadn't he mentioned the bouquet of tulips?

True, their conversation had been interrupted by the phone call. Maybe Jasper would have told Jarrod about the black flowers if he hadn't raced out of the coffee shop in such a hurry.

Or maybe Jasper had it all wrong. After all, the identity of someone who'd had a certain phone number thirty years ago was a strange motive for murder. Especially since Isabelle could have found the answer on her own. She didn't need to hire a detective to call the phone company or search through old reverse directories. So why had she?

Jasper had also mentioned birth certificates. Was that information worth his brother's life? Worth Isabelle's? In hindsight, Jarrod wanted to kick himself for not asking Isabelle about the documents.

Something sinister was going on here. Jarrod's intelligence experience, first in the military and then with his own security company, cautioned him from jumping to any conclusions without more facts. He wouldn't link the break-in, the childish threats, and the shooting until he had the evidence to do so. With his brother's life on the line, Jarrod couldn't afford to make any mistakes in his assessments.

As he headed to Jasper's office to join Captain Palmer, someone called his name. Jarrod stopped and turned around.

David "Dax" Benedict, his colleague and longtime friend, loped toward him. "One of the guys caught the chatter on the police scanner. What's going on?"

"Jasper got shot." The enormity of the simple words pressed against Jarrod's throat. He'd been able to maintain a professional facade since he arrived on the scene. But it slipped when he said the words out loud.

Dax clapped Jarrod's shoulder. "I'm sorry, boss. How is he?"

"Breathing." A heavy sigh followed. "Unconscious."

"Did they apprehend the shooter?"

"No." Jarrod took a deep breath to recover his composure. This wasn't the time to fall apart like a sandcastle at high tide. In his profession, the time to fall apart was *never*. He had a job to do. Justice for his brother demanded he do it—and do it well.

"Any idea what happened?"

"According to the only witness, Jasper's client, the shooter aimed at her." Jarrod swallowed hard, debating what to say next. How could he best express his brother's heroism without idealizing or downplaying it? Though what did it matter? Dax would understand what he meant even if he flubbed the words. He might as well keep it simple. "She says Jasper saved her life."

Dax nodded. "I can believe it."

"Me too."

"But?" Dax asked.

"I don't know," Jarrod said. He lowered his voice. "What if she's mistaken? Jasper could still be in danger. Captain Palmer had a squad car accompany his ambulance. An officer will be posted outside his room. But I still don't like it."

"I can arrange more security," Dax offered. "In fact, I'll go myself."

"I appreciate that." The weight of worry pressing against Jarrod's shoulders eased a little. He didn't expect the shooter to show up at the hospital. But then again, he'd never expected Jasper to be attacked in his own office. At least with Dax on guard, Jarrod could focus on assessing the scene while it was fresh.

"I'm going to talk to the captain," Jarrod said. "Then I'll figure out what else Jasper might have been investigating." Surely, he had a more serious case than one involving an old phone number and a couple of birth certificates. Though it wouldn't hurt to get a look at those documents. Without more information, he'd be foolish to discount Isabelle's claim that she was the target.

"Keep an eye on the client too," Jarrod said. "Her name is Isabelle Byrnes. That was her ambulance that just left."

"Leave it to me." Dax gave Jarrod a one-armed hug. "You and Jasper are in my prayers."

Jarrod's throat tightened, and he merely nodded his thanks. Coming from Dax, an intrepid warrior with a huge heart, the sentiment wasn't an empty one. Dax's prayers had seemed to pull them out of tricky situations before. No one on the team doubted his direct connection to God. Jarrod needed that comfort now.

After Dax left, Jarrod returned to Jasper's office.

Captain Palmer motioned him to a quiet corner away from the crime techs. "Anything you can tell me about what might have happened here?"

Jarrod respected Palmer as a competent and experienced officer. He'd even offered Palmer a position on his own security team before Palmer's recent promotion to captain. Palmer had refused the offer, even after Jarrod sweetened it with the promise of a generous signing bonus. "I bleed blue," Palmer had said at the time. "Family tradition."

But even though Palmer followed in his dad's and granddad's footsteps, he wasn't a seasoned investigator, and this case was personal. Besides, Jarrod wouldn't take the chance—unlikely as it might be—of classified details being leaked on the evening news, or worse, social media. "Did you interview the witness?" he asked, hoping he sounded even and detached.

"Did you?" Palmer retorted. Obviously, the captain wasn't going to let Jarrod deflect his initial question.

Jarrod mentally reviewed the conversation he'd had with Isabelle. How could he know that anything he repeated to the captain wasn't breaking confidentiality? "Ms. Byrnes is still Jasper's client and entitled to her privacy."

"She's not entitled to hinder an official investigation." Palmer's tone became sterner, but his expression remained sympathetic. "Neither are you."

"I wouldn't dream of it."

"Good." Palmer gestured toward Jasper's desk. "Might be something on that computer, though."

Jarrod ran his hand over his face and let out a sigh. No way could he hand over Jasper's computer, an older desktop, to the local police department. But he didn't want to appear antagonistic. "Might be. Do you mind if I take a look?"

Palmer hesitated as if to consider the request, then called to a crime scene tech hovering near the desk. "Hey, Jonesy. Okay if we access the computer?"

Jonesy glanced up from the photos he was flipping through on his digital camera. "Sure thing." He stepped away from the desk, his attention still focused on the photos.

Jarrod should have taken his own photos or asked Dax to do so before he left for the hospital. *I need to pull myself together. I'm better than this.*

When Jarrod learned Jasper had been shot, a worrisome fog had stretched dark fingers into his brain. That could lead him to make mistakes. And a mistake could mean Jasper's shooter escaping justice.

Jarrod slid onto the thinly padded chair and rolled closer to the desk. As he waited for the computer to boot up, he searched the drawers. He didn't find anything of interest beyond a treasure trove of assorted candy. It was better than the cliché bottle of scotch seen in too many detective novels and old noir movies. He absentmindedly unwrapped a piece and popped it into his mouth as the computer screen lit up and displayed a password box.

Jarrod went through the usual password possibilities—birth dates of family members, Jasper and Olivia's anniversary, the word *password*, their mother's maiden name, the name of their first dog, and so on. Nothing worked. Apparently, Jasper's lackadaisical approach to office security was offset by his scrupulous attention to protecting his computer from being accessed. Time to switch to plan B.

"I have a whiz kid on staff with the skills to get into this thing," Jarrod said to Palmer. "I can get him down here or take the computer to him. Your call."

As before, Palmer took his time before answering. "I'll take it to the precinct," he finally said. "He can meet me there."

"To the precinct? I'm not so sure—" Jarrod's phone buzzed. "It's Olivia. I have to take this."

"Does she know?" Palmer asked.

"I called her earlier." It had been one of the hardest calls he'd ever made in his life. To her credit, his sister-in-law had quickly recovered from her initial shock. At least she'd put up a brave front while Jarrod did his best to comfort her. "She's probably calling from the hospital. She was heading straight there."

"Hopefully, she has good news," Palmer said.

Jarrod nodded as he retreated to a quiet corner. He skipped the usual pleasantries as he answered the phone. "How is he?"

"Not good." A tremor affected Olivia's words.

Jarrod imagined her standing outside Jasper's room, one arm hooked around her waist as if that simple gesture could prevent her from falling apart. She was a strong woman, feisty even—she had to be to tolerate Jasper's crazy hours and crazier escapades—but she'd never faced anything like this before.

"He needs blood," Olivia said. "And there's not enough on hand."

Jarrod hung his head. Why hadn't that possibility occurred to him? He should have gone to the hospital immediately instead of staying at the crime scene. "I'm on my way. Everything's going to be fine." *Please, God, let everything be fine.*

He pocketed his phone and found Captain Palmer talking to another officer. "I've got to go to the hospital. Jasper needs blood."

Palmer furrowed his brows. "The hospital's short on blood?"

"We're both A negative. It's not the rarest type, but it's rare enough." Jarrod started to leave, then paused and gestured toward the desk. "Jasper's computer?"

"I'll take it to my office," Palmer said.

"Okay, but no one else touches it," Jarrod warned. "Only my guy."

"You've got my word." Palmer gave him a friendly push. "Now go. I'll see you there soon."

Jarrod took one last look at the scene, imprinting as many details as he could in his mind, and sprinted to his SUV.

As he sped to the hospital, he was flooded with memories. In one, he was an eighteen-year-old kid, impetuous and invulnerable. Or so he'd thought. On a buddy's dare, he'd "borrowed" Jasper's motorcycle and crashed in a ditch after he'd swerved to avoid a dog running across the road.

When Jarrod ended up in the ER, he'd learned that he and his older brother shared the same blood type. Confined to that hospital bed, feeling lousy from his physical injuries and even lousier for wrecking Jasper's bike, Jarrod hadn't wanted to see anyone.

But Jasper had ignored Jarrod's plea to be left alone. He'd donated his blood and stayed with Jarrod throughout that first long night. He'd been a steady and welcome presence as the forlorn hours clicked by.

"Your life is more important to me than that bike," Jasper had said in his quiet, big-brother tone. "And I'd give you my last drop of blood if you needed it. But when you're out of here, we're going to have a sit-down."

The accident had been a turning point for Jarrod, and the sit-down had ended with a trip to the local army recruiting station.

Jarrod owed his life—and more—to his brother. Now it was time for him to repay the favor.

"My last drop," he whispered.

Jarrod prayed he wouldn't be too late to save his brother.

"All I need is a hot shower and a good night's sleep," Isabelle told herself as the nurse left the room after recording her vitals. But she didn't know if she could do either without reliving the nightmare that had occurred right before her eyes. She shivered as she pulled the thin blanket to her chin.

Isabelle also needed this horrible headache to go away. The dull ache at the base of her neck had started during the ambulance trip. She'd tried to relax, but the horror of what she'd experienced wouldn't let her.

She longed to get out of here and go home. Not that going home was an option. She owed it to Jasper to find out who had shot him.

Her bloodstained clothes were folded on a nearby chair. To exit the hospital, she'd have to put them on again.

She wasn't sure she could.

Neither could she leave wearing nothing but a flimsy gown and skid-free socks.

As Isabelle pondered her options, focusing on her wardrobe choices to avoid thinking about Jasper, the door opened.

A young woman entered, an electronic tablet tucked against her chest and a pleasant smile on her face. She wore gray slacks and a matching jacket over a red blouse. A hospital ID hung from a lanyard around her neck. "I'm Lanie from the business office," she announced in a cheery voice. "I need to get some information from you if that's okay."

Isabelle welcomed the distraction. Somehow her purse had managed to accompany her to the hospital. She pulled out her driver's license and health insurance card.

Lanie scanned the items. "Is there anyone here with you? In the waiting room?"

"No." The admission caused almost as much pain as the throbbing in her head. If this had happened a few short months ago, her father would have come to pick her up, probably with a fresh change of clothing. On the other hand, if he were still alive, Isabelle wouldn't be here in the first place. She forced a smile. "It's just me."

"And your bodyguard."

Isabelle peered around Lanie toward the door, but she didn't see anyone. "I have a bodyguard?"

Lanie leaned forward and whispered conspiratorially, "A handsome one too."

"Why?"

Lanie shrugged. "He was born that way, I suppose."

Isabelle gave her a quizzical look, then realized Lanie had misunderstood her question. Too weary to explain what she'd meant, Isabelle closed her eyes. The police captain must have decided she needed protection. But from what? Or—even scarier to contemplate—from whom?

"Is there a relative I can call for you?" Lanie asked.

Only Heather. "I'll call someone," Isabelle said.

"Wonderful. Let me know if there's anything else I can do for you." Her business completed, Lanie left the room.

Isabelle pulled out her phone and stared at the screen. How could she ever explain this situation to her stepmother?

She would've already talked to her dad. His calm assurance would have eased the headache and the tension in her shoulders. Without him, she didn't feel the urgency to call anyone.

But Heather deserved to hear a firsthand account of the shooting from Isabelle instead of a secondhand account on the news. Isabelle could downplay the entire incident to keep her stepmother from worrying. Not that her efforts would keep the woman from dramatizing the event. As soon as they hung up, Heather was sure to share the awful story with all her friends so she could revel in their sympathies. Tears would be shed, mostly by Heather, even as she basked in the reflected glory of having her stepdaughter practically murdered a few short weeks after her husband's untimely death.

"Maybe I'm being too harsh," Isabelle muttered. But in her heart of hearts, she didn't think so.

Still, the call had to be made. She found Heather's name under the tab for favorites—though Heather definitely wasn't a favorite, she was still family—and pressed the screen.

The phone rang a couple of times before Heather answered, characteristically breathless and rushed. "I'm so glad you called, but I can't talk long. The Kings invited me over for some kind of social gathering. I tried to refuse. After all, you and I are still in mourning, aren't we? But they insisted, and it is for a good cause. Surely no one could object to my being there. It's not like they're throwing a cocktail party. If that were the case, I would have insisted on staying home with a good book. Laurel Johnson—do you remember her? Not that it matters. Anyway, she suggested a book the other day, and I've been meaning to download it onto my tablet. Now what was the name of it?"

At the pause, Isabelle jumped in. "I have something to tell you."

"Of course you do, and here I've been blathering on. But seriously, I have to get going soon so I'm not late. Besides, if you're going to tell me you found out anything about those birth certificates, then I simply don't want to hear it. You know I don't agree with stirring up the past."

"Someone shot at me."

Silence.

"Did you hear me?" Isabelle asked.

"I'm not sure."

Isabelle had to hold back a sudden urge to cry. At least she had gotten Heather to stop babbling. "Someone shot at me."

"But you're okay?" Heather sounded genuinely concerned. "You're not . . ."

"I'm fine." Isabelle couldn't stop the shaking in her voice as her mind flashed back to the masked woman entering through the side door, the revolver pointed at her. In Isabelle's memory, the gun's barrel overshadowed everything else, larger in her mind than it could have possibly been in the woman's double-handed grip. "I'm at the ER. Apparently, that's routine."

"Why would someone shoot at you?" Heather sounded as if she doubted Isabelle was telling her the truth.

Annoyed with the unspoken insinuation, Isabelle snapped, "She may have been aiming at someone else."

"She? Who is she?" Heather let out an exasperated breath. "I knew going off on a wild-goose chase was a bad idea. What would your father say? You need to come home. Tonight."

At the mention of her father, Isabelle's grip on her self-control wavered. But then she had to swallow an unexpected urge to laugh at Heather's unreasonable command. "I don't know that I'm up to driving. Besides, I need to stay here. To figure out why someone wants me d—" She couldn't say the word. It was too awful, too insane. To the best of her knowledge, she had no enemies. Certainly no one who wanted to end her life.

The throbbing in her head ratcheted up its pace, thumping in her temples. This was all too much.

"Then I'll come to you." Heather's no-nonsense tone was final.

"What? No, that's not necessary." Isabelle thought quickly, desperate to find a reason to keep Heather away. "Besides, like I said, I might not have been the target."

"Who else could it have been?"

"I was meeting with a private investigator," Isabelle explained. "We were at his office."

"And someone tried to kill him?"

"I don't know. It all happened so fast."

"It's too late for me to back out on the Kings," Heather said. "They're sticklers for etiquette. But I'll be there tomorrow. Send me your address."

"I already gave it to you in the note I left."

"I don't have it with me. Just send it."

Isabelle reluctantly agreed, then texted the information while Heather prattled on about being beyond fashionably late to the Kings' house, also tossing in random words of concern for Isabelle.

Someone knocked at her door. Jarrod stood there, rubbing a bandage wrapped around his arm. Worry deepened the furrows around his eyes, and his unkempt hair gave him a haggard appearance.

Isabelle smiled apologetically as she pointed at the phone. As soon as Heather paused to take a breath, Isabelle cut in. "Someone's here. I've got to go."

"If the doctor is attractive, make sure you smile pretty and let him see you're not wearing a wedding ring. Who knows? Maybe this will all turn out to be a love story. Wouldn't that be romantic? You fall in love with the man of your dreams who you would have never met if you hadn't gotten shot."

Isabelle started to tell Heather that she hadn't been shot, but she gave up. What was the use? By the time Heather retold the story to her friends, Isabelle would probably be on the brink of death. The Kings and their guests were going to be amazed at her miraculous recovery when she returned home.

"See you tomorrow," Heather said brightly. "Until then, try to stay out of trouble."

Before Isabelle could respond, the call ended. She stashed the phone in her purse and leaned back on the pillow.

"Boyfriend?" Jarrod asked, a sympathetic smile cutting through his five-o'clock shadow.

Isabelle forgot that Jasper's brother stood at her door, and she nearly jumped out of her skin when he spoke. "Stepmother." She sat up, trying to slow the pounding of her heart. "How's Jasper?"

His expression clouded. "He's in surgery."

"I'm so sorry." The words were trite, a platitude she'd abhorred when repeated again and again by the mourners at her father's funeral. But what other words were there for such a time? "I mean it. I pray he comes through this."

"We appreciate that." Jarrod stepped to the foot of the bed. "And any information you can provide to help us find out who did this."

"Are you working with the police?"

"I own a security company. We sometimes provide support for the local LEOs. When we can help."

"Leos?"

"Sorry." A small smile materialized on Jarrod's handsome face. "I guess acronyms are an occupational hazard. LEOs as in L-E-O. Law enforcement officers."

"Of course." Isabelle rubbed her temples. "My mind's a little fuzzy."

"That's to be expected. You've gone through a horrible ordeal."

She motioned to the bandage. "What happened?"

"I donated blood," he said in an offhanded manner.

But Isabelle sensed something deeper, something vulnerable,

beneath the simple sentence. He was no longer the in-control guy she'd met at Jasper's office. A helplessness he probably wasn't accustomed to feeling bowed his shoulders and softened his features.

An unexpected twinge electrified Isabelle's skin, a feeling she hadn't experienced since her college days. Her first true love was a wonderful man with a steady mind and wanderlust in his heart. He had yearned to travel to the world's out-of-the-way places with a camera in one hand and a journal in the other, while Isabelle longed to explore the past from the comfort of a stable home.

The inevitable breakup was amicable yet heartrending. Isabelle had only dated sporadically since then, hoping to experience that same heady rush again someday. She'd never expected to feel it in circumstances like this. It must be an overdose of adrenaline. Or an aftereffect from the shooting.

Her cheeks warmed with the realization she'd held his gaze a beat too long, and Jarrod seemed caught in the moment too.

Isabelle blinked, then rubbed her inner arm, as if in sympathy with him, hardly knowing what she was doing or why. "I don't want to stay here any longer," she whispered.

"It's the safest place for you."

"Someone from the business office was in here earlier. She said I have a bodyguard."

"That's Dax. He's with me. The second-best man in my company." He grinned as he waited for her to ask the obvious question.

Smiling, she took the bait. "Who's the best? Wait. I think I know the answer."

They both chuckled, and for a time the earlier horror was set aside. But neither of them could keep it at bay for long.

"Is your stepmother coming here?" Jarrod asked.

"That's what she says. But not until tomorrow."

"You don't sound too enthused."

"She means well," Isabelle said.

"But?"

But I don't want her here. She'll smother me with her notion of care and concern, which means I'll be taking more care of her than she will of me.

The thoughts shot through Isabelle's mind, words she wished she could say to someone who'd understand. Words she couldn't say to a stranger.

"But I'm fine on my own." Her voice sounded chipper. Falsely so.

"What about your father?"

Isabelle plucked at a loose thread on the blanket. The stigma of telling a stranger about her stepmother disappeared, and the comfort of telling this particular stranger about her father drew her in.

Jarrod took a step closer and perched on the edge of the bed. The understanding in his eyes gently prompted her to share her pain.

"He died a few weeks ago." Her voice, though quiet, didn't waver. "A sudden heart attack."

"You were close?"

"Very." Isabelle focused her attention on the whiteboard, the sole item of interest in this windowless room. Today's date was written in bright red letters in one corner. A pain chart with a range of smiling and frowning faces decorated one side.

"I'm sorry for your loss," he said.

"Almost every morning, he jogged along the shoreline. I usually ran with him, but I had a client meeting that morning, so . . ." Her voice trailed off, and she swallowed the lump pressing against her throat. "He didn't come back."

If only Isabelle had gone with him. Despite the coroner's assurances that Dad hadn't suffered, she couldn't push aside her regret that she hadn't been with him that day. Even if she hadn't been able to save him, at least he wouldn't have died alone.

Jarrod bent his head, a simple gesture that allowed Isabelle the space she needed to turn aside from her overwhelming grief.

"I know it's hard," he said after a long silence. "Jasper and I lost our parents during my senior year of high school. A car accident."

"How awful." Isabelle studied him—the angle of his unkempt hair against his temple, the solid line of his jaw. He'd known grief as devastating as her own. Now his brother was fighting for his life.

Had her curiosity brought this tragedy to him? Perhaps she should tell him about the birth certificates. But if Isabelle were to blame for Jasper's injuries, then telling Jarrod about the documents might put his life in danger too.

And if anything happened to him because of her, how could she ever forgive herself?

6

Jarrod left Isabelle's room when the ER physician arrived to review her chart. He'd stayed much longer than he'd intended. For reasons he couldn't explain and didn't have time to explore, he was drawn to this attractive young woman who had demonstrated such courage despite her fear. Despite the heartbreak that still shadowed her from her father's death.

He'd gone to see Isabelle to interrogate her, hoping she would give him more information than she'd given Captain Palmer. But regardless of his desperate need to know what she was hiding—and he was certain she was hiding something—he couldn't bring himself to question her.

It had been a long time since Jarrod had been undone by a pretty woman. Something about the single dimple that appeared whenever she smiled made him want to take her in his arms and make sure nothing would rob her of her dimpled grin again.

Now was not the time for adolescent fantasies. Not when Jasper's life—perhaps even Isabelle's life—was at stake.

He found Olivia with her sister, Margot, in a small waiting area in the surgical wing. They sat near a window where the afternoon sun spotlighted the worry that pulled on Olivia's face and circled her eyes. She and Jasper had been in their late twenties when they married, and their two boys had come along soon after. The perfect family.

Jarrod's family.

He took a seat beside Olivia and wrapped his arm around her shoulder. "Do the boys know?"

"Mom and Dad got them out of school," Margot answered. "They'll bring them by later. When we know more."

"I didn't want them to see him right away," Olivia explained, her voice cracking. "I didn't want them to see the blood. He lost so much blood."

"He's going to be fine," Margot told her sister, then glanced away as if unsure her words would prove true.

They sat in silence until a nurse approached to escort them to the recovery room. Jarrod and Margot stood back to allow Olivia a few private moments with her husband.

When she motioned for them to join her, Jarrod stared at his brother's ashen complexion, needing to reassure himself that Jasper was still breathing.

He found himself hypnotized by the monitor displaying Jasper's heart rate, blood pressure, and respiration. As if his energetic, outgoing, at times pompous brother were no more than sets of numbers and lines on a graph.

Jarrod squeezed Jasper's hand. The flesh was warm but unresponsive as he lay beneath a taut blanket, his chest slowly rising and falling. The tubes might be frightening, especially for his six-year-old son, but at least neither boy had seen their dad sprawled on the floor while blood flowed from his chest.

The tubes and monitors would fill their memories. But not the blood.

Jarrod placed his hand against his own chest as if feeling his brother's pain. Even his motorcycle injuries, serious as they were, couldn't compare to what Jasper must have suffered.

Suffered because someone wanted him dead? Or suffered because Jasper had risked his life to save Isabelle as she claimed?

Jarrod wished he knew. But Isabelle's perspective was simply that—her perspective. He didn't think she was lying. In fact, he was certain she believed what she was saying. But surely Jasper had more enemies around here than a complete stranger.

Time dragged, but eventually Jasper was moved to a private room in the intensive care unit. Though he was still unconscious, the prognosis was favorable.

The family gathered once again in a waiting area.

Jarrod gave Olivia a brotherly hug. "It's been a long day. How about I do a coffee run?"

"I'd like that," Olivia said.

"Already taken care of," a voice boomed. Olivia's father, Dale Pike, came toward them, carrying a drink tray with steaming cups.

Jarrod took the tray so Dale could embrace his daughter.

"Is Mom here too?" Olivia asked, her voice muffled against Dale's chest.

"She's home with the boys," Dale answered. "But don't you worry about them. When I left, they were making their own pizzas and debating which movie to watch first."

Jarrod handed out the coffee while Dale hugged Margot. Then he clasped Jarrod's upper arm and pulled him a few steps away. "You doing okay, son?"

Son. Jarrod never wanted anyone to call him that except for this man who had accepted him as one of his family from the day Jasper had asked for Olivia's hand.

Jarrod had held his emotions and his fear for his brother in check so far. But now, those emotions threatened to overwhelm him. He feigned a smile. "As well as I can, sir."

"You know we're here for you," Dale said. "Anything you need."

"I just need to find out who did this. And why."

Dale nodded. "You will. I have no doubt about it."

The older man's warm confidence boosted Jarrod's spirits, even though he wasn't sure he was worthy of it. His own dad had made a point of making sure his sons never got too big for their britches. Both Jarrod and Jasper had to find their own confidence and competence without a father's support.

Then he'd died before either of them could prove themselves to him. Jarrod still wasn't sure if that lessened or strengthened his grief. With the perspective of adulthood, he'd come to realize that his father's assessment had more to do with his own lack of confidence. That he'd wanted his sons to accomplish more than he'd been able to in his life. The realization didn't make the pain of rejection, of never measuring up, go away. But it had freed Jarrod from searching for something he'd never find.

The younger, impulsive Jarrod would be solving this case to prove something to his father. The more experienced Jarrod was solving it for Jasper. He couldn't allow anyone to get away with shooting his brother. Even if the bullet was meant for someone else, Jarrod would bring the shooter to justice.

If Jasper regained consciousness, maybe he could fill in a few missing pieces of the puzzle. *No, when. When he regained consciousness.*

"Why don't we take a walk?" Dale suggested.

Jarrod went with him to the front lobby. They chose chairs in a quiet corner where no one could hear their conversation.

"Do you have any idea who did this?" Dale asked.

"Jasper called me right before the shooting." Jarrod described how Isabelle told him about Jasper and his arrival at the crime scene.

Dax and Isabelle entered the lobby. She wore medical scrubs with her heels, and her hair was pulled into a long ponytail. Her eyes were puffy, and weariness weighed her shoulders.

When her gaze met Jarrod's, she stopped. She glanced at Dale, then back at Jarrod again. Apparently unsure whether to join them, she simply stared at him.

Jarrod motioned to Dax. "Dale, I think you know Dax."

The two men shook hands.

"This is Isabelle Byrnes, the young woman I was telling you about," Jarrod continued. "She called 911 and did everything she could to stop Jasper from bleeding out. Isabelle, this is Jasper's father-in-law, Dale Pike."

"Thank you for what you did." Dale gently took her hand in both of his. "Were you injured too?"

"No, only frightened." A small smile curved the edges of her lips, enough for the single dimple to make a brief appearance. "How is Jasper?"

"He made it through surgery," Jarrod replied. "Now we have to wait and see."

"I'm praying for him." She returned her attention to Dale. "I truly am sorry."

"Thank you," he answered. "Your presence of mind may have saved Jasper's life."

Isabelle's features clouded.

Jarrod understood what she was thinking as surely as if she'd said the words out loud: *Or I caused him to be shot.*

"I'm glad I ran into you," Isabelle said to Jarrod. "I've been discharged so I'm free to leave. Without a bodyguard."

"She doesn't want my company, boss," Dax said.

"I appreciate the kind offer, but I'll be fine. If you'll all excuse me, I'd better go." She headed for the exit.

"Wait a minute," Jarrod said, following her. "Where are you going?"

"My car is at Jasper's office. I need to pick it up."

He touched her arm, and they both stopped near the sliding glass doors. "How are you getting there?"

Isabelle pulled a piece of paper from a pocket. "A nurse gave me instructions on which trolley to take."

"You're taking the trolley?"

"It's faster than walking."

Jarrod ran his fingers along his face and sighed. The island's municipal council had decided twenty years ago that buses didn't fit the image they wanted to portray to the tourists or the locals. Too noisy, too smelly, too monstrous. Instead, they chose trolleys as their public transportation of choice—ones equipped with suitable tires so they could operate on the island streets.

"You're being incredibly foolish." As soon as the words left his mouth, he wished them back.

"Excuse me?" Isabelle demanded, glaring at him.

"Think about it," Jarrod said in a conciliatory tone. "You think the shooter meant to kill you, and now you want to ride around the island on a trolley as if you're on vacation? Let me drive you."

She studied Dale and Dax, who were near enough to overhear the conversation, as if she were assessing the men, Jarrod's offer, and the situation. "You're needed here."

Jarrod rubbed the bandage covering his arm. "I've done what I can. Besides, it won't take long. I'll be back before I'm missed."

"Let him drive you," Dale said. His tone was kind. "I think we'd all feel better knowing you had someone with you."

Isabelle hesitated, but the expression that flickered across her face told Jarrod that she was secretly, perhaps unconsciously, grateful for the offer. Maybe she wasn't as keen on riding the trolley as she wanted them to believe.

"We only want you to be safe," Jarrod said quietly.

"I appreciate that." She shrugged.

Jarrod thought her slight gesture didn't indicate indecisiveness but something more intentional. He imagined she was secure in herself but didn't want to appear overconfident to others. A gesture he found appealing.

"Okay," Isabelle said. "I'll go with you."

Before they left, Dale promised to call Jarrod immediately if there was any change in Jasper's condition. Then Dale and Dax headed back to the intensive care wing.

Jarrod and Isabelle drove to Jasper's office in silence. He had the radio turned to an all-volunteer public station with a variety of shows. Most focused on a particular musical genre, but a few had a discussion format. Jarrod enjoyed the variety.

A program featuring acoustic guitar musicians was on. The host shared historical context and interesting trivia between selections. It was one of Jarrod's favorite programs.

The current musical selection was soft and yearning, a composition Jarrod hadn't heard before. But he found it hard to focus on the finer points of the piece when his mind was overwhelmed with concern for his brother and his heart was beating faster with Isabelle sitting in the passenger seat.

This wasn't the time to analyze the strange feelings he experienced in her presence. Sure, she was attractive. Beautiful even. But he'd been around beautiful women before—dated quite a few of them—without having his heart skip a beat at her sudden arrival in a hospital lobby or when he touched her elbow as they walked across the parking lot to his car.

For her part, Isabelle stared out the passenger window. The glow of the streetlights briefly flashed over her features as Jarrod drove, and when he passed them her face was plunged into shadow again. Light, dark, light, dark. She seemed oblivious to the changes.

When they arrived at Jasper's office, Jarrod parked behind a police cruiser. Despite the increasing darkness, two officers milled around the front of the building. The crime scene techs were loading their totes and utility bins into their mobile van as Jarrod and Isabelle exited the car.

Jarrod approached one of the techs. He knew it was a long shot, but he had to ask. "Find anything interesting?"

"You know I can't answer that," the tech said.

"Sorry," a nearby officer said to Jarrod. "You'll have to wait for the reports like the rest of us."

Before Jarrod could respond, the officer's mike crackled. The voice said something about a possible B and E followed by an address.

Isabelle suddenly dug her fingers into Jarrod's arm. "What's a B and E?"

"Breaking and entering," Jarrod said.

She gripped his arm even tighter, but her focus was on the officer. "The address. What was it again?"

He repeated it, and Isabelle ran for her car.

Jarrod hesitated, then raced after her. He caught up before she opened the driver's door. "Where are you going?"

"The cottage." Her words were forceful, yet her tone was fearful. "That's the address where I'm staying."

Jarrod shook his head. It was as if his mind couldn't make sense of what his ears had heard. "Are you sure?"

"Positive."

"Come with me." He grabbed her hand and pulled her to his car.

The cruiser, sirens blaring, pulled away from the curb, with Jarrod right behind it.

His mind churned. Maybe Isabelle's perspective wasn't wrong after all. But if she was mixed up in something diabolical enough to get his brother shot, then Jarrod was determined to find out her secrets.

And to bring Jasper's shooter to justice.

From the passenger seat of Jarrod's SUV, Isabelle scanned the road ahead and wished she were more familiar with the route to the cottage. The island was long and narrow, but the streets seemed to have a logic of their own. It was as if they followed ancient trails—perhaps those made by the land's early inhabitants—instead of a pattern or grid.

The police cruiser's siren, already muted because of the incessant downpour, faded as they fell farther behind.

Jarrod hunched over the steering wheel, but without a siren of his own, he had to stop at a couple of traffic lights. His impatience was palpable.

And almost as intense as hers.

Isabelle had been so surprised when he took her hand and towed her toward his car that she hadn't resisted his pull. Sliding into his vehicle had felt like the most natural thing to do under the circumstances.

Now that a few moments had passed, she had mixed feelings about not driving her own car. She didn't like leaving it at the office, but Jarrod's familiarity with the island gave him an advantage. He didn't need to rely on a navigational app to find his way to the cottage.

Isabelle closed her eyes in a vain attempt to sort out her anxious thoughts. The truth was she was glad to be with Jarrod. After all, how smart would it be to return to the cottage by herself? Sure, the two officers were definitely going to arrive first. But she didn't know them. She didn't really know Jarrod either, but at least he was Jasper's brother so she could trust him.

Couldn't she?

She studied Jarrod. His expression was stern as he focused on his driving while the wipers swept swaths of rain from the windshield. Sometime during the day, the tropical storm must have traveled closer to the coast.

Perhaps Jarrod sensed Isabelle's attentive stare. He glanced at her. "Are you okay?"

"I feel like I'm in an episode of *The Twilight Zone*." She couldn't help smiling. "Or maybe this island is an offshoot of the Bermuda Triangle."

"I've lived here all my life," he said, "and I can promise you that I've never known a day like today."

Isabelle peered through the passenger window. Most of the shops had closed for the evening. Their lighted window displays were blurred by the heavy rain. A diner on the corner was still open, but not many people remained inside. "Maybe I should have stayed home."

Though that hadn't been an option, not when she desperately needed to know the truth about the birth certificates and why her father had hidden them.

"Don't blame yourself," Jarrod said. "We don't know what's going on yet. But I promise you, we will."

The certainty in his voice wrapped her troubled spirit in a warm blanket of hope. Isabelle *did* trust him, she admitted to herself. And not simply because he was Jasper's brother. Her regard for him went deeper than that. Perhaps too deep.

What could she say? The man exuded confidence, and more than that, he was competent. In the face of tragedy, seeing his brother lying in a pool of blood, Jarrod had managed to stay calm, swallowing the overwhelming emotions that must have been threatening to swamp him. Even while dealing with her own turmoil, Isabelle had admired Jarrod for his composure. He reminded her of her father, a man others respected because of his ability to assess a situation and respond appropriately.

Maybe that was why she'd experienced those unexpected twinges when he'd visited her at the ER and again when they talked in the hospital lobby. Somehow, in a way she couldn't explain, being near Jarrod made her miss her father even more while also softening her heartache.

For the thousandth time, she wished Dad were here. He'd know exactly what to do, what to advise her to do to stay safe. Now she only had herself to rely on.

Though maybe she also had Jarrod.

Maybe.

Isabelle gripped the door handle as Jarrod swung around a sharp curve.

"Hang on," he said. "We're almost there."

She merely nodded, staring through the windshield in her search for landmarks. She finally recognized the pink market on the corner where she'd bought a few groceries that morning. How long ago that seemed—as if days had passed since her shopping trip instead of a few hours.

"There it is." Isabelle pointed at a crosswalk. "The street leads to the ocean." A fact he probably already knew.

"Got it."

She leaned forward as far as her seat belt would allow. The lights from two police cruisers rotated in the stormy darkness. Seeing the cruisers in front of her rented cottage transformed the surreal nightmare into a bleak reality. Her quiet yet fulfilling life of genealogical research and community social functions had been upended by circumstances beyond her control.

So had Jarrod's. All because of her search for answers.

"I'm sorry you got dragged into this mess," Isabelle said. "You should be at the hospital with Jasper instead of here with me."

"This is where Jasper would want me to be." Jarrod slowed to navigate between the parked cars on the narrow street. "Where he'd expect me to be. Doing my job."

His job? Yes, that was what Isabelle was to him. A clue to the mystery of who shot his brother. A piece of a mysterious puzzle. *Get a grip*, she chided herself. *Of course that's what I am to him.*

The cruisers were parked at opposite angles, blocking the driveway. The sirens were finally silent, the lights spinning. Despite the rain, a few neighbors stood in their yards. Isabelle imagined it was a spectacle rarely seen on this quiet island.

Jarrod pulled to the side of the street in front of the cottage and shut off the ignition.

Isabelle reached for the door handle.

He touched her arm. "Maybe you should stay in the car until we know what happened."

She gaped at him. He couldn't be serious. "Are *you* staying in the car?"

Jarrod narrowed his eyes. "I'm a trained security expert. Are you?"

Surprised and more than a little irked, Isabelle pulled on the door handle. "I'm not staying in the car."

They stared at each other in a battle of wills for what felt like an eternity.

When Isabelle didn't back down, Jarrod tilted his head. He continued to hold the stare, but he relaxed the hard set of his jaw. "I can do this all day. I bested Jasper every time he dared me to a staring contest when we were kids. These days I best my nephews."

"Not fair." Isabelle blinked. "I didn't have siblings to practice on."

At least she hadn't thought so. Until now. The same questions that had rattled around in her head for the past few days taunted her again. What if everything she thought she knew was a lie? What if that older birth certificate belonged to a brother she didn't know she had? Which meant the second certificate belonged to her. How could that be when she'd inherited her dad's single dimple? No matter how many thousands of times she asked the questions, she was no closer to an answer for any of them. At least, none she was willing to accept.

Isabelle pushed the door open. Rain seeped in, quickly soaking her arm and shoulder. "I'm not staying in the car." The sentence was the same but not her tone. This time, the words lacked her earlier conviction and strength.

"Stay close to me." A nerve-tingling warmth replaced his earlier sternness. "And if I tell you to run or to drop—"

"Drop?"

"Yeah, drop. You drop to the ground. No questions, no hesitation. You understand?"

"I understand."

Jarrod opened the glove box and removed a revolver.

Isabelle gasped. "Do you always keep that there?"

"I never use it unless I have to. Are you ready to go inside?"

She tore her gaze from the gun to search his expression. His features were set in a chiseled hardness that definitely meant business, yet his eyes were soft. Gentle even.

Courage. Confidence. Competence.

All the traits she admired in her fictional heroes but had never expected to find in one man in real life.

She nodded. "I'm ready."

They walked to the cottage's stoop together.

Officer Torres greeted them, a skeptical glint in her eyes. "What are you doing here?"

"I'm renting this place," Isabelle said. "What happened?"

"One of the neighbors called 911 when he saw someone sneaking along the hedges," the officer said. "He checked the door and noticed the lock had been broken."

"Can we go inside?" Jarrod asked.

"Sure," Officer Torres replied. "We'll need to know if anything is missing."

"I arrived just a few days ago," Isabelle said. "There's a huge television mounted on the wall and the usual furniture. I don't know if I can tell you if something small has been taken. Unless it was my laptop. I left it on the dining room table."

"I don't remember seeing it there," Officer Torres said.

Isabelle stepped inside the cozy living room. The cottage was small and tidy.

The second officer stood near the entrance to the dining room, talking on his cell phone. He waved her in while he moved into the kitchen.

"It's gone." Isabelle's stomach plummeted. "My laptop is gone."

"Are you sure this is where you left it?" Jarrod asked.

"Positive. I was working on a project for a client. The files were next to it." Isabelle rounded the bare table and checked the floor. "My briefcase is gone too."

"What kind of project?" Jarrod asked her.

"A confidential one."

"I think you need to tell us," Officer Torres said. "It may be important to the case."

Isabelle pressed her fingertips to her temples. How could so much be going wrong? This particular project was too sensitive to share with anyone. She'd had to sign a confidentiality contract that was much more comprehensive than the ones she usually presented to her clients before taking on a project.

"I can't say anything until I talk to my attorney," Isabelle responded. The fear of breaching her confidentiality contract wasn't her only concern. How could she ever tell her client that the papers that she'd been entrusted with had been stolen? The horror weakened her knees. Her reputation would be ruined.

"Then you should make that call soon." Officer Torres gave Isabelle an apologetic look. "After everything else that happened today, Captain Palmer will want answers."

"She's right," Jarrod said to Isabelle. "Does that project have anything to do with why you hired my brother? If it does, then I need to know about it too." His tone practically challenged her to disagree.

"It doesn't." Isabelle turned from him, summoning all her willpower to stay upright. The last thing she wanted to do was collapse like some damsel in distress.

"There's something else I want you to see," Officer Torres said. "Follow me." She led them down the short hallway to the larger of the two bedrooms.

The light was on, though Isabelle knew it hadn't been when she left. She had planned to return to the cottage hours ago, after her planned meeting with Jasper and long before it got dark.

Isabelle entered the room, gasped, and placed both hands over her mouth. Black tulip petals were scattered all over the pale-blue comforter and along the floor into the tiny bathroom. She started forward as if pulled by an invisible hand to follow the trail of flowers.

Jarrod restrained her with a light grip on her arm, then faced the officer. "Are they in the bathroom?"

"Yes," Officer Torres said as she tapped the screen on her phone. "And there's a message."

Isabelle was afraid to ask, but she did anyway. "What does it say?"

Silently, the officer held out her phone so they could see the photo she'd taken.

On the mirror written in red lipstick were the words, *Stop now or else!*

Jarrod read the message on the phone screen. The writing appeared amateurish, even childish. "Okay if I take a look?" he asked Officer Torres.

"Don't step on any of the petals," she warned.

"I want to see it," Isabelle said.

"Are you sure?" Jarrod asked.

"If someone is sending me messages, I think I have the right."

"Same warning." Officer Torres pocketed her phone. "Watch where you step."

Jarrod gingerly stepped over the petals and peeked inside the bathroom. Black petals were scattered in the basin beneath the mirror.

"That's my favorite lipstick." Isabelle stood behind him on tiptoe and peered over his shoulder. Irritation colored her voice. The open tube rested beside the faucet handle, the tip smashed into a blunt mess. "And my most expensive."

Jarrod gently prodded her back to the bedroom. "You seem more upset about the lipstick than the message."

"I am upset." She threw up her arms and plopped down on the edge of the bed. "And angry and confused and scared. None of this makes any sense."

"Maybe not to you," Jarrod said, keeping his voice calm. Perhaps he could use this incident to win her trust and to finally get the answers he needed. "But it makes sense to someone. I think it's time you told me why you hired my brother."

Isabelle didn't answer. Instead, she rose and left the room.

Jarrod followed her to the kitchen.

As Isabelle passed the second officer, she paused. "Is it okay if I use the stove? I'd like a cup of tea."

"Is anything missing from the kitchen?" he asked.

Jarrod leaned against the doorway while Isabelle gazed around the square room. The counter space was minimal as the appliances took up most of the space.

"Not that I can tell," she replied.

"Okay, go ahead," the officer said. "Mind if I ask a few questions?"

Jarrod made himself as inconspicuous as possible. He wanted to hear this conversation.

Isabelle answered the officer's questions while preparing the tea. She removed four cups and saucers from a cupboard along with an assortment of flavored teas.

The officer held up his hand. "None for me or Officer Torres. As soon as we gather the evidence, we'll be on our way."

A flicker of fear crossed her features.

"I'll patrol past here throughout the night," the officer quickly reassured her.

"I'd appreciate that. Thank you." Isabelle turned to the stove, but her shoulders remained tense.

Jarrod could tell that Isabelle wanted to be brave, but she was frightened to stay at the cottage. Not that he could blame her. Though it was doubtful the intruder would return—most burglars weren't interested in confronting their victims—the feelings of being violated were very real. No one liked to think that someone they didn't know had been in their home, touching their personal items, while they were away. Home was supposed to be a haven. Even when the home was a vacation rental. A break-in shattered that illusion.

If Isabelle was merely a burglary victim, Jarrod wouldn't be too worried about her safety. But if the burglar was also the shooter, then she might still be in danger.

He tuned back into the conversation when the officer asked Isabelle about her missing items. To her knowledge, the burglar hadn't taken anything other than her laptop and briefcase. But she refused to go into detail about her client's project.

"The briefcase contained files and documents, along with my planner, ink pens, and a notebook," Isabelle said.

Jarrod studied her as she pulled in her lip, an unconscious gesture that might indicate she was stopping herself from saying more. She was definitely hiding something.

The officer obviously sensed it too. "If you want this perpetrator caught and your belongings returned, then you should give us as much information as possible."

The kettle whistled, and Isabelle removed it from the heat. "I understand."

From the tone of her voice, she planned to be as stubborn with the officer as she had been with Jarrod. Which only made him more determined to gain her confidence.

"Officer Torres and I will be out of your way as soon as we can," the officer said, then left the room.

"Tea?" Isabelle asked Jarrod. She gestured at the tea holder with her free hand as she poured boiling water into two cups. "I like to keep a range of them on hand. Help yourself."

Jarrod joined her at the counter and perused the options. "My grandmother loved a variety of teas. She told me she had two choices— Lipton and Earl Grey—when she was growing up. Then she and my grandfather went on vacation to North Carolina, and she discovered a tea shop in Asheville. No more Lipton and Earl Grey for her. In fact, she became quite the tea connoisseur. Or a tea snob, as Gramps used to say."

A small smile tilted the corners of her lips, and her eyes sparkled.

"What?" Was she making fun of him? Why had he even told her that story anyway? He never talked about his personal life with strangers. Despite the forced intimacy between them due to recent events, Isabelle remained a stranger.

"I love stories like that," Isabelle said. "The anecdotes that say so much about a person, about what is important to them. About what's important to you."

"Tea isn't important to me. I don't really care for it." Jarrod held up a bag of chai tea. "See? It's all flavored hot water to me—nothing more."

"What would your grandmother say about such heresy?" Her voice sounded strained beneath her teasing tone, as if she were trying to lighten the tension created by the day's strange circumstances. "Besides, the tea isn't important. The memories of your grandmother are what matter."

"True." Jarrod chuckled. "I said that to her once, about tea being flavored hot water. She swatted me with a towel." He rubbed his thigh. "I can still feel the sting."

Isabelle grinned. "I think I would have liked your grandmother."

"She would have liked you too. I imagine she'd have told you all kinds of family anecdotes over a cup of steaming hot orange ginger."

"That's my favorite. How did you know?"

He was taken aback. "Orange ginger? You're kidding."

"I absolutely love it," she said. "But a quality combo can be hard to find."

"I know. I used to special order it for Grams. It was her favorite as well." Out of all the flavors of tea in the world, what were the odds that Isabelle and Grams had the same favorite?

An unexpected charge raced up Jarrod's spine, the kind that usually warned him to be on his guard or take extra precautions. Except there was a warmth to this charge. Instead of making him hypervigilant, the feeling encouraged him to relax.

Not a feeling he was used to experiencing.

It was definitely time to change the subject, but Jarrod wasn't ready to interrogate Isabelle again. At least not yet. If he bombarded her with questions, she'd no doubt put up an impenetrable wall between them.

Once again, he needed to give her a reason to trust him.

While they waited for the officers to finish their work, Jarrod asked Isabelle about her interest in genealogy, keeping the conversation light and nonintrusive. He couldn't help being charmed as Isabelle grew more animated. Maybe he should research his own family tree someday.

Officer Torres entered the kitchen. "We're heading out. Are you going to be okay?"

"She will be," Jarrod interjected, then gave Isabelle an apologetic smile. "I understand you don't want to be a nuisance to anyone, but I'd rather not spend the night staked out front. My company has a safe house where you can stay. Do me a favor and say yes."

"Staked out front?" Isabelle gave him a puzzled frown. "I'd never expect you to do that. You should return to the hospital or go home and get a good night's sleep."

"That's not going to happen if you stay here," he said. "Jasper would want me to keep you safe."

Isabelle's steady gaze seemed to pierce his thoughts.

But Jarrod didn't waver in returning it. He was telling her the truth, and if she was as perceptive as he believed her to be, she would see that.

After a moment or two, Isabelle faced Officer Torres. "What's your professional opinion?"

The officer chuckled. "I can vouch for Jarrod's character, if that's what you're asking. All things considered, you should take him up on his offer."

"Thank you." Isabelle carried the tea things to the sink. "I believe you're right."

Jarrod widened his eyes. He'd expected more of a fight. "You mean it?"

"I want to be brave," Isabelle reluctantly admitted. "But I won't be able to sleep here. I'm not sure I'll sleep anywhere."

"I promise I can keep you safe." He pulled out his phone. "I just need to make a call."

Isabelle released a deep breath, then squared her shoulders. "I'll pack a bag."

"Take your time." Jarrod sounded almost giddy with relief, like a schoolboy who expected to be rebuffed by the popular girl but found himself taking her to the prom.

He shook his head. Where had that silly analogy come from? He'd never had trouble getting a date to the prom or any other important event.

Besides, Jarrod needed to stay professional. In charge. To be the man with a plan.

Except he didn't have a plan. For now, all he could do was protect Isabelle.

And he realized with a start that he'd give his life to do that.

Jarrod gave Isabelle a quick tour of the safe house, the apartment above the garage of one of his military buddies, then checked the kitchen to be sure the fridge and pantry were stocked with the essentials. Half a gallon of milk, a carton of eggs, assorted condiments. Coffee pods and a few other items. Not much but enough to get by.

She'd changed into jeans and a long-sleeved T-shirt before they left the cottage rental.

He tamped down the attraction her appearance stirred within him. After all, this wasn't a date but an assignment. Except that wasn't right either. Isabelle was Jasper's client, not his. Yet it was his responsibility to guard her, to keep her safe. A responsibility he relished because it kept his worry about Jasper at bay. And because—crazy as it sounded considering they'd met that day—he couldn't bear the thought of anything happening to her.

Nothing would. Not as long as he had breath.

"Nice place," she remarked. "Thanks for bringing me here."

"Thanks for agreeing to come." Jarrod gestured toward the living area. "Could we talk for a moment before I go?"

"You're going to ask me again, aren't you?"

"I am."

Isabelle gave an exaggerated sigh before sinking into the soft cushions of an upholstered chair.

He sat opposite her and leaned forward, elbows on his knees. "I understand all about client confidentiality. In my business, that's paramount. I wouldn't ask you to break it if my brother hadn't been shot today. If there's anything more you can tell me, anything at all, I need to know."

"I didn't hire Jasper on behalf of one of my clients," she admitted, "The case was more personal."

Finally, Jarrod was making progress. He maintained his casual demeanor, hoping she'd continue to open up to him. "He mentioned birth certificates. Who do they belong to?"

"He told you?" Isabelle fidgeted in the chair, drawing her legs up beneath her, then letting one dangle.

"Only that they exist. No details." He pressed his lips together, giving her time to gather her thoughts. To fill the silence.

"A few days ago, I went through the items in my father's safe," she said softly. "I thought I knew everything he kept in there, but I was wrong."

Jarrod straightened and pressed his palms against his knees. "You found the birth certificates?"

"One for a boy and one for a girl." Isabelle bent her head, apparently engrossed in her cuticles. "The girl's birth date is the same as mine."

"Who are they?"

She regarded him with something akin to defiance. "No names for the children on either one. No father's name. They had the mother's name, though."

"I take it the name wasn't your mother's."

"No."

"You were adopted?"

"I never thought so. In fact, I resemble my father. Same hair, same solitary dimple." Isabelle pointed to her cheek and gave him a smile that didn't reach her eyes.

He returned her smile with a brief one of his own. That solitary dimple would steal his heart if he wasn't careful. "Then maybe the birth date is a coincidence."

"I don't know." She blinked back tears. "That's why I hired Jasper."

"What about the phone number?"

"It was written on the back of one of the certificates," Isabelle said. "In my dad's handwriting."

"Can you tell me about him?" Jarrod asked.

He listened attentively as Isabelle talked about her father. She obviously adored the man, and their relationship had grown even closer after the loss of her mother. The new stepmother had changed the family dynamics—no surprise there—but not Isabelle's regard for her dad. Fortunately, Heather didn't seem interested in driving a wedge between the father and the daughter. At least, that was the impression Jarrod was getting as Isabelle opened up about her family.

Eventually the conversation returned to the birth certificates.

"Jasper had discovered the identity of the baby boy," Isabelle said. "That's why I was at his office."

"Who is he?"

"He didn't get the chance to tell me." She sniffled. "When I went to his office, the lock on the door was broken. I walked inside and found everything a mess. I called Jasper. He arrived not long before that woman appeared. You know the rest."

Jarrod realized that Jasper had abruptly left the coffee shop because of Isabelle's call. "What about the birth certificates? Are they missing?"

Isabelle opened her mouth, then closed it again. Her nod was barely perceptible. "But I have copies. I scanned the birth certificates to send to Jasper before we met." She tapped her phone's screen and handed the device to Jarrod.

He zoomed in on the documents. "Michelle Blacke. Do you know who she is?"

"No idea. Our family attorney has never heard of her."

Jarrod studied the pictures, committing them to memory. He didn't want to ask the obvious question, but surely it was one that Isabelle had already considered.

"No," she said.

"I didn't say anything."

"You were going to." She stared at him. "And the answer is no. My dad didn't cheat on my mother."

"It happens."

"Not with them."

He decided not to push the argument. Doing so would alienate her, and he needed her on his side, not holding a grudge because he didn't believe her dad was a saint.

If Michelle Blacke had been involved with Isabelle's dad, then that truth would eventually be revealed. Nothing Jarrod or Isabelle could do would change that. It was better to focus on what they knew to be facts without forming any preconceived conclusions.

"Let's talk this through," Jarrod said. "What is it with these tulip petals?"

"I wish I knew." Her eyes brightened. "Perhaps this Michelle Blacke has something to do with them. Her last name is Blacke. Black tulip petals."

"I suppose there could be a connection." Yet it was almost too obvious. Again, he couldn't shake the feeling that a cold-blooded killer wouldn't bother with tulips and messages. Unless the shooter hadn't intended to hit anyone. Perhaps she'd merely meant to send a stronger message.

Or perhaps the incidents weren't related but simply an unlikely coincidence.

"Someone breaks into Jasper's office," Jarrod said, needing to talk through the day's events, "and steals the files pertaining to your case, along with other files. Someone sneaks into Jasper's office and shoots him. Someone breaks into your rental cottage and steals your laptop and briefcase. A thief. A shooter. A thief. That's what we know. What we don't know is if it was the same thief both times and if the thief is also the shooter."

"You think there are two, maybe three, different people involved?" Isabelle sounded incredulous. "That seems unlikely."

"I agree." Unless they were all working together, though even that was a crazy idea. "But we can't eliminate any possibilities until we know for sure. Not if we want answers."

"None of it makes sense to me," she said. "Even if I'm Baby Girl Blacke, who would care? My parents—whether they are my biological parents or my adoptive parents—are both dead. I just found those birth certificates a few days ago. Hardly anyone knows I even have them."

Jarrod perked up while castigating himself for not asking that basic question sooner. "That's where we begin. Who knows about the birth certificates?"

"Heather and our attorney, Reuben Hart, were with me when I found them. But they were as surprised as I was."

"How did they react?"

"Heather wanted to burn them," Isabelle said with no small amount of annoyance. "She's afraid of unknown heirs trying to get their hands on my father's estate."

"It's a common motive," he replied.

"True. Though Heather received a specific inheritance according to her prenuptial agreement—a percentage of the estate—she's afraid her share will be tied up in an ongoing court case if relatives come around."

"What about this Hart fellow?"

"Reuben advised that it was best to leave the past alone," she answered, "He said I might not like what I discovered."

"He has a point." Jarrod propped his elbows on his knees and gazed at Isabelle. He could get lost in the beauty of her eyes if he didn't watch himself. Her earnestness and quiet confidence appealed to a vulnerability within him that he needed to ignore if he wanted to solve this case. "Maybe he knows more than you think."

"No," Isabelle said firmly. "My father trusted Reuben with his business ventures while he was a lawyer, his charitable outreach when he was a judge, and every aspect of our estate."

"But not with his deepest secret?"

"I promise you that Reuben was shocked. In fact, I think he was hurt that Dad hadn't confided in him."

He rubbed his palms against his legs and leaned back. "Did you tell anyone else?"

"Jasper," she said. "But that's it."

"So those are our prime suspects." Jarrod snorted. "Your father's trophy wife, the family's loyal retainer, and the shady private investigator."

"You're being cynical," Isabelle accused.

"Am I?"

"Granted, Heather has all the trappings of a trophy wife, but she's not an evil person. Reuben is almost a member of the family. And I know you don't consider your brother to be shady."

"You're right," he said. "Jasper's anything but shady. Still, there's that old saying. I think it comes from a Sherlock Holmes story."

"Something about when you have eliminated the impossible, then whatever remains, even if it's improbable, is the truth?"

"That's the one." Jarrod stood, feeling as if his energy had recharged during the conversation and needed an outlet. He strode to the double doors that led to a small balcony on one side of the garage and peeked through a gap in the closed vertical blinds. Rain pelted against the glass, reducing visibility to near zero.

"I think you're so upset about your brother that you're seeing everyone as a suspect," Isabelle said. "You probably even suspect me."

"I did at first," he admitted. At her stricken expression, he laughed. "But I quickly crossed you off the list."

"Why?"

"An educated hunch." He shoved his hands into his pockets. "And my doubts that you could fake the horror you were feeling while you did everything humanly possible to save Jasper's life."

Her face blanched, and she stared at her hands.

Jarrod noticed that she'd washed her hands at the rental cottage and here at the safe house as if she could still see, or perhaps feel, Jasper's blood on her skin. Another reason he didn't believe she could be the shooter.

Though that didn't mean she wasn't involved in the thefts. But what would have been the point? Isabelle had discovered birth certificates and wanted to know whose they were. She had no reason to steal anything.

"I'm going to go now." He'd already stayed away from the hospital too long, and he had a long to-do list. He needed to check with his tech guy about Jasper's computer and run background checks on Heather Byrnes and Reuben Hart despite Isabelle's belief in their innocence. And most importantly, he needed to retrace Jasper's steps in his investigation of the birth certificates.

If Jasper could find out Baby Boy Blacke's identity, then so could Jarrod.

Isabelle rose from the chair to accompany him to the door.

He ran through his final instructions, though what he wanted to do was pull her into his arms until the world turned right side up again.

"Set the security alarm after I leave." Jarrod opened the contacts on his phone. "What's your number?"

She hesitated a moment, then recited it for him.

He added the info and sent her a text. "Now you have my number. If you need me, just call. No matter the time. No matter the reason."

"Thank you, but I'm sure I'll be fine." Isabelle infused cheerful optimism into her tone. "It's been a long day. I'll probably fall fast asleep."

"Hopefully, you will." Jarrod started to pocket his phone when it rang. He checked the screen. "It's my sister-in-law."

The instant the call connected, Olivia's voice came through the speaker, her words rushed and frantic. "Where are you? Something has gone wrong. We need you."

9

After a restless night's sleep filled with disturbing dreams of her blood-smeared hands cradling black tulip petals, Isabelle rose before daybreak and took a long shower. The heat of the water soothed her frayed nerves and relaxed her tense muscles.

Despite her weariness and the mild throbbing of a headache, she resisted the temptation to crawl back under the covers. Instead, she dressed in comfy sweatpants and a Jacksonville Jaguars sweatshirt, then wandered into the living area and opened the vertical blinds.

The sky was beginning to lighten with the promise of a new day. One that would no doubt grow dark again if the tropical storm brewing in the Atlantic swirled closer to land. Hopefully, it wouldn't strengthen into a hurricane.

After a series of hurricanes hit Florida, her father had renovated an inner room of the mansion to provide a modicum of comfort and appropriate shelter during major storms. Fortunately, the family had needed it only a few times.

But where would Isabelle find shelter on this island if the storm worsened? If it stalled offshore for a few more days, maybe she'd be home before it made landfall. Though she had no intention of leaving until the mystery of the black petals and Jasper's shooter was solved.

Isabelle peered again at the pale-gray clouds. As peaceful as the sky appeared, it was difficult to imagine a storm of any magnitude threatened them. But that was typical of Florida's atypical weather.

Some of her favorite days were when the sun shone even while rain poured from delightfully blue skies.

She checked her phone, but Jarrod hadn't called or texted. Not that she'd expected him to since she wasn't family or even a close friend. But she was deeply concerned about Jasper and had hoped for an update. The disappointment of not hearing from Jarrod settled like a stone in her stomach. A heavier stone than the situation warranted—one that led to heartwarming thoughts that felt utterly inappropriate to indulge in, given the circumstances.

What a ridiculous time for romantic ideas. She told herself that it wasn't romance but rather an understandable emotional reaction to the man who offered her security when she needed it most. But she had to repeat it too often for it to be completely believable.

Isabelle curled up in the corner of the couch, positioned to enjoy the view outside the patio doors. Chubby brown squirrels chased one another up and around the massive trunks and limbs of a laurel oak and a red maple that had been planted too close together. Their branches intermingled, as tangled as it now seemed her family tree might be. It was a strange thought to contemplate since she'd always considered her genealogical record to be straightforward and uncomplicated.

The information about their earliest known ancestors had come from the ancient family Bible enclosed in a glass display table near one wall of shelves in Dad's spacious office. Isabelle's great-grandfather, an avid genealogist, had confirmed that information with his own research that traced the family's migration to the New World in the early 1800s and the slow movement south from New York to Richmond to Charleston to Saint Augustine.

Isabelle's grandfather had transferred the contents of the cardboard boxes he'd inherited from his father to leather-bound books with high-quality archival sheet protectors. Those books had inspired Isabelle's own love of genealogy and family history, leading to her profession as a genealogical researcher and archivist.

She'd studied the books as a teen and used them as a resource for her senior project. Compared to many families, her tree was thin and long-reaching. This person married so-and-so. These children were born. They married or not. Had children or not. They died, and the next generation continued the cycle. But there were no mysteries. No fatherless children, at least not in the line of her direct ancestry, and no secret births.

Isabelle drew a soft afghan around her shoulders and rested her head against the back of the couch. Her eyelids grew heavy while the sun's rays lightened the outside world. Thoughts of playful squirrels and intertwined leaves quieted her mind as she drifted into blissful and much-needed sleep.

A knock on the door startled her awake. She sat up, unsure where she was, and squinted against the glare of the sun. The knock came again, and she grabbed her phone to check the time. Though she felt like she had dozed for a few minutes, she'd slept for well over an hour.

Once again, someone knocked on the door.

"Coming," Isabelle called, rubbing her neck as she rose from the couch. She peered through the peephole. Jarrod stood on the landing at the top of the stairs, a leather bag hanging from one shoulder. He balanced a restaurant sack and drink container with two coffee cups.

"Just a sec." She hurriedly shut off the security alarm, unhooked the chain, and twisted the dead bolt. She turned the knob, then realized it was locked too. After fumbling with it, she yanked the door open.

"Took you long enough," Jarrod teased as he held out the sack. "Hungry?"

"This place is locked up tighter than . . ." Words failed her. *A drum* was too cliché, and so was *Fort Knox*. Why couldn't she ever come up with a witticism on the spur of the moment?

Dad would have known what to say. He had a talent for clever repartee. She'd always delighted in her father's wit, but she'd never been able to emulate it.

"That's why we call it a *safe* house." Jarrod's smile above his unshaven jaw reminded Isabelle of the Cheshire cat.

"Very clever." She laughed as she waved him in.

He set the drink carrier and restaurant sack on the table, then lowered his leather bag to a chair. "Have you eaten?"

"Not yet."

"Good. I stopped by Zapped for coffee, and they had these egg casseroles. I picked up a couple of them." Jarrod grinned. "Okay, I bought several. I wasn't sure whether you'd prefer the peppers or the bacon or the veggie version."

It was an easy decision. "Bacon for me."

He removed a carryout box from the sack. "You got it."

Isabelle retrieved tableware and napkins from the kitchen. Even though she hardly knew Jarrod, she intuited his good humor was mostly a pretense. It wasn't hard to guess why. "Were you at the hospital all night?"

Jarrod arranged the remaining boxes on one side of the table and folded the sack. He seemed to be avoiding her gaze. "Most of it."

No wonder he looked so weary. Though still amazingly handsome. "And?"

"There was a crisis. Jasper needed another surgery. He's stabilized now." His chipper facade faded away as he rubbed the back of his neck. "The doctors say he needs time. But . . ."

"The waiting is hard," she finished for him.

"Yes," he agreed, the syllable little more than a soft breath.

Isabelle understood his sense of helplessness. She'd felt the same way those last days with her mom—powerless but still clinging to hope. At least Jarrod had more hope than she had. Despite the sense that the hours dragged, death had come too soon for her mom. Death always came too soon.

"Anyway, my tech guy couldn't find anything related to your case on Jasper's computer. So I brought mine." The intimate moment abruptly ended. His tone was unnaturally upbeat, as if to hide his brief vulnerability. "My firm has access to a few databases that may help us narrow our search for the elusive Michelle Blacke. Ready to get started?"

"More than ready." Finally, they were taking action. Maybe today would be the day they'd discover the answers she needed. That they both needed.

"Great." Jarrod removed his laptop from the leather bag and gestured toward the food. "Go ahead and eat. It'll take me a few minutes to log in to a secure portal."

Isabelle hadn't realized how hungry she was until she took the first bite. She practically devoured the bacon casserole while he tapped at the keys.

He tried to hide a grin as he pushed a second carryout box toward her.

She pretended to be offended until she bit into the colorful casserole. The green, yellow, and red peppers baked into the egg-and-cheese mixture were delicious.

"Here we go," Jarrod said. "Michelle Blacke."

"Blacke with an *e*," Isabelle reminded him.

"Blacke with an *e*," he repeated as he entered the names in the correct fields. "Let's see what we can find about the baby girl first. Date of birth?"

She told him.

"County?"

"Volusia."

"Great. Second search, same mother's name. Baby boy's DOB?"

Isabelle gave him the date. "That certificate was issued in Miami-Dade County."

"Both babies were born in December." Jarrod tilted his head as if in thought. "Given the timing, I wonder if she had some spring break adventures."

"Spring break?" She paused as the realization hit. The birth dates indicated that Michelle had probably became pregnant both times in March or April, popular spring break months. "If that's the story, then Michelle might have been in her late teens or early twenties. Maybe that will help narrow the search."

"It's helpful to tighten the parameters, but it's still only a supposition," he warned. "A possibility but not a probability."

"Are you always so cautious?"

"In my line of work, caution is a strength. At least during an investigation. It's dangerous to leap to conclusions or grab hold of a theory too soon. You can miss important clues if you think you already have the answer."

While the databases ran, Jarrod opened one of the remaining casseroles and dug in, mainly focused on the screen. Despite his delayed start, he finished his meal seconds after Isabelle.

She cleared the table, stuffing the garbage into the trash can beneath the kitchen sink.

Several more minutes passed before the computer dinged.

"We've got a list," he announced. "Thirteen possible names."

"Sounds unlucky."

"You're not superstitious, are you?"

"Not usually." Isabelle flashed a self-conscious grin. "But I don't usually have people leaving me threatening messages and shooting at me either."

"I guess you have the right to be at least a little superstitious," Jarrod said. "Tell you what. We'll divide the list. I'll take seven names, and you can take six. Find their phone numbers, and give them a call."

"And say what?" Isabelle was practiced at making cold calls to possible descendants of long-dead ancestors on behalf of her clients, but she wasn't sure she could call a list of Michelle Blackes and casually inquire about their possible children. "'Hello, did you deliver a baby on this date in this county?' That's a bit intrusive, isn't it?"

"It is intrusive," he agreed. "But it's also direct. With a potential killer running around, we don't have time to beat around the bush."

She opened her mouth to object when Jarrod's phone rang. He was right, of course. And she wanted answers—she *needed* answers—as soon as possible. If this was the best way to get them, then she'd take a deep breath and make the calls.

"Say that again," Jarrod said into his phone. "I'll be right there."

The intensity of his tone caught Isabelle's attention. His face was grim. "Is it Jasper?" she asked when he hung up.

"Dax. He caught someone sneaking into Jasper's office."

Jarrod hurriedly saved the search results, sent them to his phone, and shut down his laptop.

Isabelle returned from the bedroom. Her hair was brushed into a neat ponytail. She carried sneakers and her purse.

"Going somewhere?" he asked.

"With you." She perched on the edge of the couch and laced up her shoes.

Jarrod raised an eyebrow as he packed his bag. While he disliked the notion of babysitting her in what could be a tough situation, his heart nudged him to relent. Somehow she even made the mere act of tying her shoes appear graceful. But professionalism won out. "I don't think so."

"You can't hold me hostage here," Isabelle said matter-of-factly, as if they were discussing something as benign as the weather. Though even the weather wasn't benign these days, not with a storm looming off the coast. "Besides, my car is still at Jasper's office."

"I'm not holding you hostage," he protested. He inwardly cringed at the obvious sign of weakness, responding to a nonsensical argument as if it had any validity.

"Great." She bounced off the sofa and hitched her bag over her shoulder. "Let's go."

Jarrod met her stare and tensed his facial muscles to show he meant business.

But his display of strength came too late. Isabelle responded with a smirk. She obviously didn't intend to back down, and he didn't have time to argue.

"Same rules we had last night apply. You do as I—hey!"

She was already out the door.

He grabbed his laptop bag and followed her. He liked a woman with spunk, but she could have waited for him to finish his sentence.

Jarrod caught up with Isabelle at the bottom of the stairs, but she didn't pause despite the strong winds blowing from the east. His SUV was parked in the drive, and she headed for the passenger side, bracing herself against the driving wind, while he fumbled with his key fob.

He never fumbled with his key fob.

Finally, he managed to unlock the doors. "Get in," he said more forcefully than he intended. "I don't have all day."

"Neither do I," she shot back.

They didn't speak, both apparently lost in their own thoughts. Jarrod's guilt over his rudeness didn't alleviate his frustration that Isabelle had invited herself along. Who knew what they'd find when they reached Jasper's office? Though from what Dax had said during their phone call, he had the situation under control.

"The island is beautiful," Isabelle remarked, breaking the silence. "Too bad I'm not on vacation instead."

"Do you wish you hadn't come?" Jarrod's tone was gruffer than he meant it to be, but it was too late to take it back.

"No," Isabelle said hesitantly. "And yes."

He felt her gaze upon him, as if she were assessing him.

A gentle sigh escaped her lips. "And no."

A pulse of electricity sparked Jarrod's being, tempting him to reach for Isabelle's hand, cradle her cheek in his palm, and kiss her solitary dimple. He pushed away those thoughts and cleared his throat as if preparing to say something profound when he didn't know what to say.

Except to remind himself that only a fool read more into a simple no than what it was meant to convey. But a no accompanied by the look Isabelle had given him, one he'd sensed more than seen, wasn't all that simple.

"Why no and yes and no?" Jarrod couldn't believe he was asking her that question. But something inside him needed the answer. Especially to that last no.

"No because I'm a genealogist." Isabelle shifted in her seat. "And those birth certificates are strange."

"Because of the missing information?"

"It's odd for a father's name to be omitted," she explained. "The courts usually want to know that a child will be financially provided for by both parents, and they want a father to be informed of his rights before a child is placed for adoption. Plus, Michelle Blacke didn't even name her children. It's like she didn't care about them at all."

The hurt in her voice touched a deep place in Jarrod's heart. Isabelle could claim she wanted to learn the truth because she was a genealogist, but it was clear that wasn't the entire story. Her search for answers was personal. She needed to know the secret her father had hidden from her—if she was Baby Girl Blacke.

He slowed at a traffic light and turned left. "Or she was a troubled young woman who knew she couldn't take care of a baby on her own."

"I could almost believe that if it had happened once." A pained expression crossed Isabelle's face. "But twice?"

Jarrod longed to comfort her, but he didn't know how. He didn't understand Michelle's behavior either. They would be at Jasper's office soon, and, selfish as it seemed, he was more interested right now in Isabelle's second no than her first. Not that he wanted her to know that.

No. And yes. And no.

"What about the yes?" he asked. "Why do you regret coming?"

She waved her hand. "Because of all this mayhem."

"You mean the tropical storm?" Jarrod joked. "I don't think you brought it with you."

"Not funny."

She was staring out the window again. The ends of her ponytail curled onto her shoulder. This wasn't the time to ask about the final no. Maybe that time would never come.

Jarrod parked next to Isabelle's car in the tiny lot behind Jasper's office. "Here we are. Service with a smile."

"You are such a gentleman," Isabelle responded, though she sounded strained.

"My mother insisted."

"I'd like to meet your mother."

Jarrod wished that too. "If that were possible." Sorrow pressed against the guilt and worry that already consumed him. All emotions he needed to get under control so he could do his job of finding Michelle Blacke and the woman in the mask who'd shot Jasper.

"Oh, Jarrod," Isabelle said quietly. She covered his hand with hers. "I wasn't thinking. I'm sorry."

Hearing his name was a breath of sweet air, and her gentle touch warmed his skin. Without thinking, he adjusted his hand so their fingers intertwined. Thankfully, she didn't pull away. When he spoke, his conciliatory tone matched hers. "Don't be. She would have liked you."

"The ache never quite goes away, does it?"

Jarrod turned toward her and glanced at her lips. The impulse to kiss her overwhelmed him while every instinct fought against such an unprofessional move. Instead, he quirked a smile and squeezed her hand before letting go. "Get in your car, and drive back to the safe house. Okay?"

Isabelle merely smiled, opened her door, and jogged toward the office.

Jarrod groaned as he hurried after her. She was inside before he could stop her.

He followed and found Dax and a woman he'd never seen before in the lobby. The woman sat in one of the padded chairs, legs crossed, hands clasped around her knees. Jarrod guessed she was in her early fifties, but her poise and calm demeanor gave off a younger vibe. Something about her features was familiar. Jarrod shifted his gaze from the woman to Isabelle and back again.

Despite the age difference, the resemblance between the two women was remarkable. Judging by the mixture of confusion and disbelief on Isabelle's face, she noticed it too.

He took a deep breath. "I'm Jarrod Long. And you are?"

"I'm waiting for Jasper Long," the woman replied. Her voice was smooth and polished, but it held the faint rasp of a smoker. "Are you related?"

"We're brothers."

"Are you also a private investigator?"

"Security expert." Jarrod shifted from one foot to the other. "Mind telling me why you're here?"

"I have an appointment with Jasper." She focused on Jarrod, paying no attention to Isabelle or Dax. "Is he on his way?"

"Look around." Jarrod gestured at the remnants of fingerprint powder on the surfaces and the clutter that needed to be cleaned up. "Didn't you notice the crime scene tape on the door?"

"As if anyone could miss it," the woman replied. "But as I said, I have an appointment."

"Who are you?" Isabelle blurted out.

The woman silently assessed Isabelle.

Jarrod thought the resemblance between the two women seemed even stronger as they stared at each other.

"My name is Morgan Young," she finally said.

"No," Isabelle responded. "You're Michelle Blacke. I know it." She grabbed Jarrod's arm. "We found her. I mean, Jasper must have found her." She faced the woman again. "That's why you're here, isn't it? Jasper asked you to come."

Morgan's eyes softened. "You and I have a passing resemblance, which leads me to believe you're searching for a member of your family." She stood and retrieved her bag from the floor. "I'm sorry to disappoint, but I can't help you. And since Jasper apparently won't be keeping our appointment, I must be on my way."

"Someone shot him." Jarrod moved to block her departure. "He's in the hospital."

For the first time, Morgan showed a flicker of emotion.

Surprise? Shock? Suspicion? Jarrod wasn't sure.

An instant later, Morgan regained her composure. "I didn't know," she said, her tone sympathetic. "What is his prognosis?"

"Hopeful."

"Who shot him?"

"We don't know." Jarrod took a step closer, crossed his arms, and glared at the woman. "Was it you?"

Surprisingly, Morgan took the accusation in stride as if being accused of attempted murder were a common occurrence. "Do you think I'd be here now if I had?"

"Criminals have been known to return to the scene of the crime," Jarrod observed.

"Again, I am not a fool."

"You didn't deny being a criminal," Jarrod pointed out.

"Word games. You are clever." Morgan stepped closer to Isabelle and scrutinized her once more. "The past is a mysterious place filled with bright spots and dark ones. It's great fun to revisit the former.

But disturbing the latter often leads to more heartache. Be sure you're ready to face the consequences of your search before digging too deep."

"You are Michelle Blacke," Isabelle insisted. "I know you are."

"Something isn't true simply because you want it to be," Morgan said, then addressed Jarrod. "I do hope your brother recovers. Goodbye." She walked around Jarrod.

Dax moved to the door as if to block her exit.

Jarrod caught his attention, and a silent message passed between them before Dax stood down. Perhaps Isabelle was right about Morgan's identity, but they couldn't stop her from leaving or force her to tell them anything.

Morgan continued out the door.

"Wait!" Isabelle cried out.

Morgan turned toward her.

"My name is Isabelle Byrnes. My father was Davis Byrnes. After he died, I found two birth certificates in his safe." Isabelle closed the gap between her and Morgan. "If you know anything about those certificates, about who I am, please tell me."

Jarrod scrutinized Morgan as she listened to Isabelle's plea. Her expression remained impassive, almost cold. But she blinked when Isabelle said, *My father was Davis Byrnes.*

The past tense *was* apparently had an impact Morgan couldn't ignore.

She knew more than she wanted to admit. Either something about why Jasper was shot or, more likely, something about those birth certificates. So why was she being so secretive?

Jarrod wouldn't rest until he discovered what Morgan was hiding.

Isabelle knew it was rude to stare, but she positively gaped at Morgan Young. The moment was surreal, as if she were being given a glimpse into the future. In twenty or so years, this would be the reflection she'd see in the mirror. Same oval face. Same dark eyes. All that was missing was the single dimple obviously inherited from her father. Davis Byrnes. He had to be her father. But what was his relationship to this woman? Fear swept over Isabelle once again that everything she thought she'd known about her parents, about her family, was a lie.

Her phone rang, and she tore her gaze from Morgan to check the screen. *Heather.* She'd already ignored a couple of calls from her stepmother that morning. But this wasn't a good time to answer the phone. She hit the decline button.

Mere seconds later, a text arrived. *I'm here. Where are you?*

Heather's timing couldn't have been worse. "Please don't go," Isabelle begged Morgan. "I'm asking for a few minutes of your time. For answers."

"I don't have answers," Morgan said. "I'm here on a private matter."

Isabelle's text alert beeped again. "Just give me a minute. I need to call my stepmother."

Morgan didn't answer, but neither did she move toward the door.

Isabelle took that as silent agreement to her request. She wandered into a nearby hallway and tapped on Heather's name. "This isn't a great time," she said as soon as Heather answered.

"Don't you hang up on me." Heather's irritated voice burst through the device. "I want to know what's going on."

"What do you mean?"

"Isn't this where you're staying?" Heather recited the rental cottage's address.

"Yes," Isabelle said. "But I'm not there."

"Obviously," Heather huffed. "If you were, we'd be having this conversation in person instead of over the phone. What happened here?"

"Wait a minute. Are you saying you're at the cottage?"

"I told you I was coming. Don't you remember when we talked yesterday?" Without giving Isabelle a chance to answer, Heather continued. "I know you had a bad day, but I'm here, so we can have our own girls' getaway. We've never done that before."

"I don't—"

"This place is covered with yellow tape," Heather remarked, cutting her off. "I don't understand what's going on or why you haven't called me."

Isabelle moved the phone away from her ear as Heather's volume increased.

"We only have each other now," Heather said. "You do realize that, don't you? Is this where the shooting took place?"

"Not the shooting, no," Isabelle replied, trying to keep her tone calm. "But someone broke into the cottage yesterday. I stayed somewhere else."

"Where would that be? I hope it's more suitable for someone of your social position than one of these ramshackle huts. Why would you ever rent this dump? I suppose it looked better online. You can never trust those photos and descriptions."

Isabelle thought quickly. She wasn't ready to tell Heather that she'd stayed in a safe house provided by a man she'd met the day before under dire circumstances. Her mind seized on another option. "I haven't made a reservation yet, but there's a lovely hotel on the mainland. I saw a brochure about it at one of the local restaurants." She gave her the name and address of the hotel. "You'll love it there. I'll meet you as soon as I can."

"When will that be?" Heather whined. "I've driven a long way to get here, and the weather is horrible. I hope the hotel has a lot of amenities if we're going to be stuck indoors for a few days. Though those weather experts can't make up their minds on where that storm is going to go. It could hit this island, and then what will happen to us?"

All the more reason you should have stayed home. Isabelle bit back the words she wanted to say. They wouldn't do any good, and Heather had a habit of holding a grudge. That was all Isabelle needed. Grumpy Heather was worse than a spoiled toddler who needed a nap.

"I promise I won't be long," Isabelle soothed. "I'm in a meeting, so I have to go." *Please, God, forgive me for that little white lie.*

"You haven't found out anything about those birth certificates, have you?" Heather asked. She was likely gearing up for another tirade.

Isabelle wished she had the nerve to drop the call, but she couldn't do that. At least not yet. "I'll catch you up when I see you."

"I think the best thing to do is go home," Heather said. "If we leave right now, we'll still have plenty of time to get cozy in our own comfortable space. Then it won't matter how strong this storm gets or where it lands. That's what we should do." She stopped talking as if waiting for Isabelle's agreement.

A thousand thoughts flitted through Isabelle's mind. It seemed strange that Heather drove all the way to the island simply to plead with Isabelle for them both to return home. If she wanted Isabelle to come home, why had she made the drive? A girls' getaway—something they'd never even talked about—seemed a flimsy excuse.

More likely, Heather intended to be close by in case Isabelle discovered any information about a possible sibling. And Heather probably wanted Isabelle to leave the island in hopes she'd give up the search. But that wasn't going to happen, especially now that she'd met Morgan Young. The resemblance between Isabelle and the mysterious woman couldn't be a coincidence.

"I'm not going home yet, but I'll try to join you for lunch." Isabelle felt like crossing her fingers and holding them behind her back. At least she'd said *try*, so if she didn't make it, she wouldn't have actually lied. Truth be told, she didn't want to meet up with Heather until she absolutely had to. The later in the day the better. She was in no hurry to hear a lecture on the foolishness of her quest or listen to Heather's demands that they return home.

The soft murmur of voices came from the other room.

"I have to go. Text me your room number once you get settled." Isabelle hung up without giving Heather a chance to respond, feeling a mixture of adolescent rebellion and regret at the disrespectful action.

She's not my mother.

The thought zipped through Isabelle's mind as rationale for her behavior. But it was followed by a tightening of the knot in her stomach. It was ever more likely that her mother hadn't been her mother. So who was? Michelle Blacke, the woman whose name appeared on the birth certificate that probably belonged to Isabelle? Morgan Young, the stranger with whom she shared an uncanny resemblance? Or, despite Morgan's protests, were they one and the same?

Her mind in a whirl, Isabelle returned to the others. Dax focused on his phone while Jarrod stood in the open doorway as rain pelted him.

Morgan Young was gone.

Jarrod shook rainwater from his hair and closed the office door.

Isabelle raced to the window. She gripped her phone in one hand and pressed her other palm against the glass. "You let her leave?" she asked, frustration mingling with disbelief in her voice.

"I couldn't convince her to stay," Jarrod responded. Did Isabelle think he had the authority to hold Morgan against her will? He wanted to help Isabelle discover the answers she sought, but his main concern was to find the person responsible for shooting his brother. He couldn't let Isabelle distract him from considering the possibility that her case and Jasper's shooting had nothing to do with each other.

Morgan's hesitance and cagey behavior might have something to do with Isabelle. Or she might have had an appointment with Jasper for a completely different reason—one which may or may not have caused Jasper to end up in intensive care. Right now, there were too many threads tangled together. But did they belong together? Jarrod couldn't say for sure. Not yet.

As Isabelle stared out the window, her expression changed from disbelief to resignation.

A twinge of guilt poked at Jarrod's conscience for responding to her question in such a cavalier manner. Truth was, if he could have kept Morgan here, he would have. His abrupt tone was a result of his own helplessness in the situation. But he shouldn't blame Isabelle for that.

"Don't worry," he said soothingly. "I gave her my card, and we'll try to locate her if we need to."

"She could be in Georgia in a couple of hours, and who knows where she might go from there?" Isabelle argued. "Now we'll never find out what she knows. Or who she really is."

"For the moment, we don't have any reason to doubt she's Morgan Young," Jarrod pointed out. But he had every intention of doing a deep dive into Morgan's background. Finding out everything he could about her was his top priority, taking precedence over his list of Michelle Blackes.

"I doubt her." Isabelle folded her arms, as if bracing for a fight.

Jarrod wished he could tell her that he had everything under control, which wasn't nearly as true as he'd like it to be.

"What if she flees to North Carolina or Mississippi or Illinois?" Isabelle asked, her voice rising in pitch. Clearly, she had no intention of calming down. "Even if we locate her, it won't do us any good if she refuses to talk to us."

"We have to give her a reason to want to talk to us," Jarrod said. "Then it won't matter where she is. We'll follow her to the moon if we have to."

"If you say so." Isabelle slipped her phone into her bag. "That was my stepmother who called. She went to the cottage and was worried when she saw the crime scene tape."

"Your stepmother is on the island?" That was strange, given what he'd gathered about their relationship. Though he shouldn't be surprised Isabelle would want the comfort of a familiar face—whatever their relationship—after all she'd experienced in the past twenty-four hours. Heather could give Isabelle the solace he couldn't. "That's good," he said, offering her a smile.

A cloud flickered across her face.

"Or maybe not so good?" he asked slowly.

"She means well," Isabelle said with a sigh. "I suggested she check in at a hotel on the mainland. I'm supposed to meet her there."

Relief and dread battled inside Jarrod. Relief that Isabelle was leaving, meaning he'd be able to do his job without the distraction of her presence. Dread that she wasn't staying, that they wouldn't be working together to seek the answers they both needed.

Isabelle was obviously waiting for him to say something, but words failed him. He didn't want her to go, but he couldn't ask her to stay.

She rummaged through her bag for her car keys. "I'll try to find the contact info for the women on my list, but I doubt I'll be able to make any phone calls with Heather in the room. I'd prefer to wait until we know the identities of those babies before telling her anything we've learned." Her tone deepened with sadness. "I realize that's probably asking the impossible."

"Probably," Jarrod said. "Though I'm sure she's only concerned about your welfare."

Isabelle gave him a sad smile. "You mean the welfare of my bank account. And hers."

"Is she really that heartless?"

"No," she admitted. Her smile gained warmth. "Thank you for breakfast this morning. And for everything you're doing to help me out. I may not always act like it, but I am appreciative."

"I know." Two tiny words, thick with meaning beyond their simplicity. Jarrod's heart seemed to have a mind of its own when it came to this woman he'd been unaware of until she'd told him the horrible news of his brother being shot. He didn't know what to do with the ridiculous feelings she caused in him—feelings that propelled him toward her, that responded to the essence she hid deep within herself.

Neither did he understand the *why*. Why her and why now? Their current situation was the antithesis of romantic. Yet a longing as ancient as the beginning of time drew them together even as circumstances pushed them apart. He didn't understand his own heart, not when Isabelle stood before him, her soft eyes penetrating his soul.

"I'll walk you to your car," Jarrod said lamely.

"No need for both of us to get wet." Isabelle somehow made her refusal sound more like an invitation.

"I'm already wet," he said. "Besides, you might still be in danger. Maybe I should drive you to the hotel."

She stared once again into the storm. "I'm going straight there, and no one knows that except those of us in this room. I can trust both of you, right?"

"Of course you can," Jarrod said, speaking for him and Dax. "But—"

"No." Isabelle put up her hand. "I'll be fine, and you have work to do."

"If you insist." He didn't like giving in, but what other choice did he have? He couldn't keep her hostage any more than he could have kept Morgan from leaving. "But I'm still walking you to your car."

And he would still worry. Not just because she was Jasper's client but because she was slowly burrowing her way into his heart.

Once Jarrod had seen Isabelle safely to her car and she'd driven away, he returned to the office more drenched than before.

"Do you want me to tail her?" Dax asked.

"That's a good idea. Whatever you do, don't let her see you." Jarrod grabbed a towel from the bathroom and dried his hair. "On your way, call Samantha. Tell her to go to the hotel. I want a photo of this stepmother if possible." It went without saying that Samantha—another military vet who'd joined his company after her final tour—shouldn't let Heather know she was with Jarrod's security team.

His phone vibrated, and he glanced at the caller ID. It was Olivia. "Any news?"

"Jasper woke up," she said, her voice a mixture of excitement and anxiety. "He talked to me."

"That's great," Jarrod said.

"A positive sign, yes." Olivia paused and took a few deep breaths as if to calm herself. "But he was so agitated, they had to give him a sedative. It was all we could do to keep him in bed."

"That sounds like Jasper." The man was a pent-up ball of energy when he was laid up, and he'd want to get back to his open cases as soon as possible. "Did he say anything about the shooter? About what happened?"

"It was hard to understand him because he's so dopey from the painkillers. But he wanted to see you. He was very upset you weren't here." The mildest note of accusation colored Olivia's words.

It was enough to prod Jarrod's guilt that he hadn't gone to the hospital between stopping by his office to get his laptop and meeting with Isabelle at the safe house. Though he'd been at the hospital all night standing vigil. If only he'd stayed a little longer . . .

"I'm at his office now," Jarrod said, as if that explained everything when it explained nothing.

"Jasper said he had to tell you about Casey. Is that one of his clients?"

"Casey?" He didn't recall seeing that name in the current files his tech guy had salvaged. "I don't know who that is. Did he say anything else?"

"Nothing that we could make out," Olivia answered. "He's sleeping again, but he doesn't seem very peaceful. I wish you had been here."

"Me too. I'm sorry I wasn't."

"I know." She paused again. "We all want you to find who did this."

"I'll keep poking around. Casey has to be a clue." But a clue to what? They spoke a few more moments before Olivia ended the call.

Someone had stacked the ransacked file folders on the desk in a willy-nilly fashion. Jarrod started sifting through them, alert for any mention of Casey. Perhaps Casey didn't refer to a person but to something else. A place? An object? It was another example of how easy it was to jump to a conclusion instead of staying open-minded to all the possibilities.

Maybe Isabelle would know. He dug out his phone and called her, telling himself that he had a legitimate reason for calling beyond wanting to hear her voice, to be reassured she was safe.

When she answered, he got straight to the point. "I just talked to Olivia. Jasper woke up for a short time. He mentioned the word *Casey*. Does that mean anything to you?"

"Who's Casey?"

"I'm not sure Casey is a who," Jarrod replied. "Did Jasper ever mention it to you?"

"Not that I remem—oh no." Isabelle's voice went up an octave.

"You remembered something?"

"I can't—"

His muscles tensed. "Where are you?"

"On the bridge to the mainland." She sounded near tears.

Jarrod sprinted to his SUV, shouting Isabelle's name, knowing he'd never make it in time.

Isabelle screamed, and the grating sounds of metal on metal pierced the phone's speaker.

Then all was silent.

Isabelle screamed as she pumped her brakes, but her efforts were in vain. The long bridge connecting the island to the mainland, with its concrete and metal sides, gave her nowhere to go. She tried to minimize the impact as much as she could, aiming for the right rear bumper of the car in front of her. She stiffened her arms and tightened her grip on the steering wheel as she braced herself.

The jarring screech of metal against metal echoed in her ears as her car rammed into one vehicle and was hit from behind by another. The impact spun the car dangerously close to the opposite lane.

Another hit, and the car spun again, this time hurtling into the concrete barrier. Isabelle glimpsed the river through the horrendous downpour, and then a loud sound caused her ears to ring as the airbag pushed against her chest. The blow stunned her, and a sharp odor filled her nostrils.

Rain pelted the windows and the roof. Her head whirled, and she struggled to stay conscious. Her chest ached as if she'd been in a boxing match, and she wasn't sure whether she could move. Whether she should move.

Hot tears flowed down her cheeks as Isabelle tried to shut out the chaos she'd caused because of her defective brakes. What if someone was seriously injured? Worse, what if someone had died? It was an accident, but she was still at fault.

Isabelle slowly pushed the airbag away from her, but the effort cost more energy than she had to expend. She closed her eyes, and the world descended into darkness.

As Isabelle endured the taking of her vitals, she calculated the odds of being in the same ER twice in less than twenty-four hours. She was even in the same room with the same nurse.

Isabelle's neck, shoulders, and chest ached, and scrapes and bruises covered her wrists and forearms. But her ears had stopped ringing, and the dizziness had subsided. Somehow she'd managed to survive the multicar pileup without any serious harm.

The nurse left with a promise—or a threat, depending on one's outlook—to return soon.

Thankfully, in what could only be described as a miracle, no one had life-threatening injuries because of the wreck. Traffic was light and slow because of the pounding rain. But that knowledge did little to relieve Isabelle's conscience. The devastation she had caused the other victims was substantial, because of their injuries and in terms of the damage to their vehicles. She foresaw insurance claims, maybe even a lawsuit. Perhaps multiple lawsuits.

Isabelle hadn't told anyone about her failing brakes. A judge's daughter knew better than to confess to anything without consulting an attorney first. But her silence increased the heaviness of her guilt.

A knock sounded on the door, and Jarrod entered the room. His concerned expression eased into a smile. "You really didn't want to see your stepmother, did you?" he teased. His smile fell away as he took in her bandaged arms. "Are you okay?"

His worried tone warmed her in a way the heated blanket had failed to do. Perhaps, for a moment or two, she could be forgiven for relishing that warmth instead of wallowing in guilt. "I've been better."

Jarrod pulled up a chair and straddled it, draping his arms over the back. "I'm tempted to say we've got to stop meeting like this. But this is real life, not the script to a late-night B movie."

"I happen to be a fan of late-night B movies."

"A classy dame like you?" Jarrod made a great show of considering, then dismissing the idea. "No, I don't believe it."

"Not all B movies," Isabelle admitted. "But the ones from the thirties and forties are fabulous."

"Name one," Jarrod challenged.

She recalled lazy days at home with her parents when Dad would drag out his collection of classic DVDs. "Any of the old Tarzan movies with Johnny Weissmuller. Adaptations of Sherlock Holmes stories. And Roy Rogers and Dale Evans."

"Those are definitely oldies. But I've got to say, there's never been a better Tarzan than old Johnny."

"My grandparents had friends who owned a drive-in theater." Isabelle rested against the pillow, allowing her mind to drift to the pleasantness of the past. "We'd go there on Friday nights when I was young and sit in lawn chairs in front of the giant screen. Eat popcorn and get eaten by mosquitoes."

"Mosquitos. Sounds lovely." His sarcasm was softened by a warm smile.

"It was a treat to stay up so late. I don't suppose I had a care in the world back then." The wistfulness in her voice surprised her. And embarrassed her. Jarrod seemed to be a witness to all her weaknesses and vulnerabilities, but she wanted him to see her strength and professionalism.

He nodded. "We take a lot for granted when we're kids."

Neither spoke at first, as if both needed to digest the truth of his words.

When the silence grew awkward, Jarrod cleared his throat. "I expected your stepmother would be here."

"We talked." It had been an excruciating conversation. Heather had exclaimed about poor Isabelle and what a horrible thing to happen and how she didn't know why anyone would choose to drive in such weather, a comment that completely undermined her earlier argument that they should go home.

She wouldn't dare be so foolish, Heather had continued. Surely Isabelle understood that. What Isabelle understood was that Heather had no interest in leaving her comfy hotel suite to play the role of concerned parent in a dreary hospital room.

The hurt of Heather's neglect was coated with relief that the woman planned to order room service and binge-watch television until Isabelle somehow made her way to the hotel. After the loss of her father, Isabelle yearned for someone to care enough about her to rush to her side. But Heather would never be that person.

"She doesn't want to cross the bridge in this weather," Isabelle told Jarrod.

"Just as well. It's going to take time to clear the wreckage." His tone suggested he knew what Isabelle had left unsaid and meant to soothe her hurt feelings by giving Heather a legitimate excuse for not coming to the hospital.

In her heart, she silently thanked him for his prudent discretion. *Courage. Confidence. Competence.* She'd attributed those characteristics to him before. Now she added *compassion*.

Isabelle blushed when she realized she was staring at him and said the first thing that popped into her mind. "I suppose my car was totaled."

"Along with some others. Any idea what happened?"

Isabelle searched his expression. She'd had a few seconds of lucidity before being whisked from the scene by an ambulance. But Jarrod had contacts in the police department. Had investigators already determined her fault? Did he know she was to blame?

"Did you see it? All the cars . . ." At a loss for words to describe the horrific images that blurred before her, she looked away.

"By the time I got there, you were gone. But Dax was a few cars behind you."

"Dax?" Her bewilderment quickly clicked to clarity. "He was following me."

"Yeah," Jarrod admitted.

"Does he know what happened?" Isabelle plucked at the thin blanket and brushed away imaginary lint.

He clasped her hand, wrapping his warm fingers around hers. "What is it?"

"It was me," she blurted.

"You think you caused the pileup?" Jarrod sounded incredulous. "No, it was the rain and the lack of visibility. The accident wasn't your fault."

"My brakes. They didn't work. I tried and tried to stop." Isabelle gasped, unable to say anything else.

His grip on her hand tightened. "Were your brakes going bad?"

"No, I don't think so." She pulled her hand away and drew the blanket over her face to hide her shame. The chair legs rattled against the floor. Though her eyes were closed beneath the blanket, she sensed Jarrod standing over her.

He touched her shoulder, warming her with his comforting presence. "I'd like to have Dax get our mechanic to check out your car. Is that okay?"

Isabelle pulled the blanket far enough down to peer at him. His countenance was tense with worry and something deeper, something dangerous.

"You think . . ." No, it was too horrible. Too ridiculous.

"That someone tampered with your brakes?" Jarrod brushed a strand of hair from her face. "Yes, I do."

By the time Jarrod had returned from making his phone call to Dax, Isabelle had endured another visit from the doctor who proceeded to order an MRI to rule out a concussion. Another unforeseen item on today's list. She would never find Michelle Blacke as long as she was stuck in this hospital.

"Dax is taking care of everything." Jarrod handed her a pudding cup and a spoon. "Found this in the break room."

"Thanks." She appreciated the gesture, a small act of kindness, though she wasn't hungry. Even so, she pulled off the foil cover. "How did you know chocolate is my favorite?"

"Chocolate is everybody's favorite." He hovered over her, then returned to the chair, as if he had more to say but had changed his mind.

Isabelle plunged the spoon into the pudding. "How's Jasper?"

"No change."

"You should be with your family instead of babysitting me."

Jarrod rested his ankle across his knee. "Guarding, not babysitting."

"There's a difference?"

He shrugged.

Isabelle ate several bites of pudding. Apparently, she was hungrier than she'd realized. As much as she didn't want to be a burden to anyone and definitely didn't want Jarrod to think she couldn't take care of herself, she appreciated him staying with her. Even if his reason was because he needed her help to figure out what had happened to his brother.

If only she had something to tell him. But maybe . . .

"I had an idea about who Casey might be, but it's a long shot."

Jarrod indicated his interest by leaning forward. "Tell me."

"I don't want to get your hopes up," she said. "It's just that I've seen all these signs around the island."

"What signs?"

"Campaign signs." Isabelle scooped up another spoonful of pudding. "Is it possible that Jasper didn't say *Casey* but *K. C.*? As in—"

"K. C. Reid?"

"You know her?"

"I know of her," he replied. "She's a typical politician. Touts her achievements and downplays her defeats. Right now, she's one of our county commissioners, but she's running for a seat in the Florida House of Representatives. From what I understand, she's in an uphill battle. The incumbent is a popular guy."

"But what if she's 'Casey'? Maybe Jasper found out something she didn't want anyone to know."

"I suppose it's possible."

"What can you tell me about her?" she asked. "What does K. C. stand for?"

"Katherine Carolina. Quite the name, isn't it?"

"I like it," Isabelle said, her tone purposefully flippant.

At first the search for Michelle Blacke and the unknown babies she'd given life to had seemed like a well-intentioned and extremely personal genealogical adventure. Never could Isabelle have dreamed that her search would turn into such a quagmire. But as Jarrod had stressed more than once, she couldn't be sure that Jasper's wounds had anything to do with her case.

Still, after spending time in the hospital two days in a row, Isabelle was tired of thinking, tired of being scared, tired of the guilt pressing against her because of the accident and the shooting. Maybe she and Jarrod could talk about something else for a few minutes, so she could pretend her life was still normal and dull.

This Katherine Carolina—whether she was the K. C. or Casey mentioned by Jasper—might be the distraction both of them needed.

"What else do you know about her?" Isabelle asked.

"She was a district attorney before she got into politics," Jarrod answered. "Thomas Reid, her husband, is a real estate agent. Between them, they're involved with everything—historical preservation board, gardening club, chamber of commerce—and seem to be doing well financially."

"What makes you think so?"

"I'll show you." He dug his phone from his pocket, tapped the screen several times, and passed the phone to Isabelle. "Here's K. C.'s campaign website. There are photos of her and Thomas, their house, and the grounds. Big place on the southern end of the island, which is known for its landscaping. They own other properties that they rent out. In fact, they might own that place where you were staying."

Isabelle regarded the photo of a large house. "I haven't seen any other two-story houses on the island. I guess I haven't driven around enough."

"There aren't many," Jarrod said. "Most of the houses were built in the late forties and early fifties. A lot of World War II veterans who'd spent time in Florida's training camps settled here after the war. For the most part, they built modest three-bedroom, one-bathroom homes. Thomas and K. C.'s house was built fifteen or twenty years ago. If I remember right, the original owner bought two adjoining lots, bulldozed the existing houses, and started over."

"It's a beautiful home," she commented.

"More suited for an Ocala horse farm if you ask me," he said dismissively.

Isabelle frowned. She could see his point. The island was too small and intimate for such a sprawling house and grounds. But it would be perfect as the main house on a country estate of a few hundred acres surrounded by the white fences often used to mark the boundaries of horse properties.

She couldn't help wondering if Jarrod was a property snob who preferred modest cottages. What would he say about her mansion? He'd probably never want to live in such a place.

The frown deepened. Where had the idea come from that such a thing would ever happen?

Isabelle returned her attention to the site and tapped on a photo of a husband and wife. She zoomed in on the photo and gasped.

"What is it?" Jarrod asked.

She studied the husband, scarcely able to believe what she saw. "This is Thomas Reid?"

He glanced at the phone. "Sure is. Do you know him?"

Isabelle stared at the man's face in the picture, drawn by his deep-set gray eyes and the single dimple in his lower left cheek.

"What's wrong?" Jarrod tapped her arm. "Talk to me."

She tore her gaze from the photo. "Thomas Reid is the spitting image of my dad."

Jarrod gaped at Isabelle. Her dark eyes were wide with shock, and her skin paled beneath the lingering bronze of her summer tan. Her abrupt declaration didn't make sense. He felt as discombobulated as if she'd provided proof that two plus two equaled five.

He didn't want to believe her, but the incredulity that rolled off her in waves convinced him that what she said was true. Yet how could Thomas Reid be related to Isabelle's father?

Jarrod and Thomas were close in age and had played on the same high school sports teams. They'd hung out with different crowds, but their mothers had served together on a few school and civic committees, so they'd been on friendly terms.

"Do you think..." Isabelle couldn't seem to bring herself to finish her question.

But she didn't need to because Jarrod could complete it for her. What if Davis Byrnes was Thomas's father? But then who was Michelle Blacke? And what part did Morgan Young play in the family?

Jarrod couldn't recall hearing any gossip about Thomas being adopted. But why would he? Maybe an adoption was common knowledge, and Jarrod had never given it a thought. After all, as a teenager, why would he have cared?

Isabelle studied the picture again. "I've seen photos of my dad when he was younger. The resemblance is uncanny."

Before Jarrod could respond, a nurse pushed a wheelchair into the room. "Time for that MRI," she chirped.

Isabelle frowned as she handed Jarrod his phone.

"I'll be in Jasper's room," he said. "Let me know when you're ready to leave, and I'll drive you to the hotel."

"You don't need to do that," Isabelle responded. "I can take a cab."

The sadness in her voice, as if her entire world had been turned topsy-turvy, tugged at Jarrod's heart. He wanted to reach for her hand again, link his fingers with hers, and let her know she could draw strength from him. As much as she needed for as long as she needed.

But he couldn't, not in front of the smiling, too-observant nurse.

"We've had this argument before." Jarrod tried to inject humor into his tone, but he wasn't sure he succeeded. "And see what happened when you got your way?"

Isabelle shot him a look.

He responded with a lopsided grin. "I'm sorry. That didn't come out the way I wanted it to."

She sighed heavily. "The MRI could take a while."

"I've got nowhere else to be." Jarrod widened his smile. "While we're on the island, maybe we could stop at the safe house first. I need to make a few phone calls."

After Isabelle reluctantly agreed to go with him, he excused himself and left the room. While he waited for her to undergo the test and be released, he'd sit with Jasper. Perhaps his brother would wake up, and Jarrod could ask him if *Casey* referred to K. C. Reid.

It was a vain hope, but it was the only hope he had at the moment.

Jarrod itched to get on his laptop, but the research would have to wait. He sat next to Jasper's bed, acutely aware of the machines that monitored his brother's every breath, every beat of his heart as Jasper rested, his mind oblivious to his surroundings.

Once Jarrod had persuaded Olivia to take a much-needed break from her vigil, he unlocked his phone and pulled up the legal thriller e-book he was reading. "I've heard that people in a coma can sometimes hear what's going on around them. You may not be in a coma, but just in case you're listening, I'm going to read you a story. We won't get to the end, so that means you have to hang around to find out what happens to the hero."

When Olivia returned, Jarrod set his phone aside. He did his best to engage her in conversation, though neither of them had much to say that hadn't already been said. Jasper's condition remained the same, which in itself was both a blessing and a curse—the former because he wasn't getting worse, the latter because he wasn't getting better either.

When Jarrod received the text from Isabelle saying she'd meet him in the lobby, he gripped his brother's hand. "Remember what I told you. If you want to hear how that book ends, you've got to hang around."

All he got in response was the robotic beeping of the machinery all around him.

Jarrod pulled Olivia into a brotherly embrace and kissed her temple. Then he left the room and jogged toward the parking garage.

He drove his SUV under the awning that covered the front entrance. As he climbed out, he noticed Isabelle sitting in a wheelchair on the other side of the sliding glass doors. With her bowed head and slumped shoulders, she appeared defeated and vulnerable.

The desire to protect Isabelle from whoever and whatever tormented her—the writer of the threatening notes, the mysterious shooter, the grief over the loss of her dad, and the secrets left for her to find—surged through him.

Jarrod grinned, guessing that she'd hate the notion of needing a knight to rescue her. But his feelings for her weren't about being her savior. They went deeper than that. He longed to be her support in tough times and her encourager in good ones. To walk with her, beside her, along whatever path lay before them.

The inexplicable emotion Isabelle caused in him didn't make sense. He'd only known her for a day. Yet he couldn't shake it.

Jarrod grabbed a jacket from the back seat, a thick corduroy that had been left there after a camping trip, and hurried inside.

Isabelle stood as he approached, gripping the wheelchair for support.

"Are you sure you're okay?" he asked. "Maybe you should stay the night."

"Too late," she said lightly. "The papers are signed, and I'm getting out of here. The painkiller is making me tired—that's all. I'm fine."

Jarrod helped her into the oversize jacket. "When we get to the safe house, you can take a nap while I do a little research."

Isabelle's eyes sparked. "But I want to help with the investigation."

"No can do." He tugged at the jacket's collar. "You don't have the clearance for the resources I'll be accessing."

"I'm not going to sit by and twiddle my thumbs while you have all the fun."

"Would you like me to take you directly to your hotel?" Jarrod grinned. "Your stepmother can make sure you don't overexert yourself."

She groaned. "You win. Again."

"Who's keeping score?" he teased.

"I am," Isabelle said forcefully. She smiled and held his gaze for a long moment, then tucked her hands into the jacket's deep pockets.

Jarrod had to admit he liked seeing her swamped by his jacket. He placed his arm around her shoulder, alert to the slightest signal that such attention might be unwanted.

Instead, Isabelle leaned into him as they walked through the sliding glass door, as if she needed his support.

When they arrived at the safe house, Jarrod set up his laptop again on the dining table while Isabelle took a shower. During her absence, he did a search on Morgan Young. He found an address of a house located in the interior of the island within walking distance of the commercial district—if a few stores, the tiny library branch, and a gas station could be called a commercial district.

He went to the county property appraiser's site and plugged in the address. The owner was indeed Morgan Young.

That made her story more plausible. She could have an issue that required Jasper's expertise. But Jarrod trusted his gut, and his gut told him that Morgan knew something about Isabelle that she wasn't telling.

With her name and address, Jarrod found she was employed as a paralegal and had a superb credit rating.

Creating a dossier on Morgan kept his mind off Isabelle. No sounds emanated from the bedroom. Hopefully, that meant she was taking a nap.

He continued his work, making notes and delving into Morgan's history until she no longer had one. The woman hadn't existed thirty years ago. He could find nothing about her educational background or any relatives.

Jarrod turned his attention to Michelle Blacke, but she appeared to be a ghost. Maybe he should find out more about Davis Byrnes. Especially while Isabelle was out of the room.

He typed her father's name into one of the databases. When the bedroom door opened, he quickly minimized the screen and pulled up the last search he'd been conducting on Michelle Blacke.

Isabelle walked over to him. Though her movements were stiff, her eyes shone. "I talked to a friend at the Vital Statistics Office in Jacksonville—"

"Weren't you supposed to be sleeping?" Jarrod interrupted.

"I couldn't." Her entire being practically buzzed with excitement. "So I called this friend to see if she could tell me anything about Thomas Reid's birth certificate."

"And?"

"He's adopted." Isabelle rubbed her arms, and her excitement dimmed. "But the records are sealed."

Isabelle studied Jarrod as he absorbed the news of Thomas's adoption. His expression didn't change, but his eyes flickered with a calm satisfaction. Isabelle would have missed it if she hadn't been watching him, knowing what to expect.

She knew that Jarrod had been trained to keep his emotions in check and his face impassive in matters such as this. As a judge who valued the virtue of impartiality, her father had achieved the same skill. But Isabelle had learned to recognize the gleam that sparked for an instant in Dad's gray eyes when his interest was piqued. She recognized that same momentary gleam in Jarrod's hazel ones.

A wave of dizziness passed over her, and she took a seat at the table before she fell down.

Jarrod stood and reached for her.

Isabelle waved him away as she settled in the chair. The steaming shower had done wonders, and the medications took the edge off the lingering pain in her chest from the punch of the airbag. But neither obliterated the soreness in her muscles or the aches from the bruises on her arms.

"Are you okay?" he asked. "Do you need anything? Tea? Water?"

Isabelle couldn't help smiling. His concern touched her. This man she barely knew showed more care for her than anyone outside the hospital. Heather didn't even know Isabelle had been released yet. Though hours had passed since they had spoken, her stepmother hadn't even bothered to send as much as a simple text asking about her.

She dismissed his questions with a shake of her head. "I simply need to sit here for a minute."

"Take your time," Jarrod said as he sat down.

Isabelle inhaled a deep breath, then let the words flow. "Thomas Reid's birth date matches the birth date on the certificate I found."

"That is extremely interesting," he mused. "Did your friend tell you anything else?"

"Like I said, the records are sealed."

Jarrod opened a new window on his laptop. "What's that date again?" He typed in the numbers she rattled off. "Looks like K. C.'s husband could be the same Thomas Reid. I've also got a social security number."

Butterflies flitted in Isabelle's stomach. Had they found Michelle Blacke's son? If so, did Thomas know anything about Michelle's daughter? The butterflies collided in a heavy mass as Isabelle's euphoric hope stumbled over another of their mysterious puzzle pieces—Thomas's strong resemblance to Davis Byrnes. Isabelle needed to know if and how the two men were related.

"We need Thomas's DNA," she said flatly.

Jarrod glanced up from his computer. "You want to ask Thomas to take a DNA test? What if he doesn't even know he's adopted?"

Isabelle leaned forward, needing Jarrod to understand the importance of her proposal. "The other option is to petition the court to open the adoption records. I don't have legal grounds to make that request."

"You can't force him to take a DNA test either," he countered.

"All I want to do is meet him." Even to her own ears, her voice sounded small and defeated. But she couldn't give up, not when the answers were so close. "If he already knows he's adopted, he might be curious about his family. Curious enough to find out if *we're* family."

"If he doesn't know, you'd be upending his life and maybe putting a wedge between him and his parents." Jarrod raked his fingers through his hair. "I'm not sure about this."

They sat in silence for a few moments.

Isabelle considered the genealogical searches she'd done that had connected her clients with unknown family members. A couple of cases had turned ugly when adults discovered the family that they'd always considered to be their own had kept their adoptions a secret. In a few other instances, adult children knew of their adoptions but had no interest in meeting their biological families. The hurt and pain in all those cases had been deep and unrelenting.

Isabelle understood the longing for answers in a way she'd never truly understood before. She didn't want to hurt Thomas or his family. But neither did she want to live the rest of her life not knowing if he was her family too. The discovery of the birth certificates had awakened an ache inside her heart that would never go away if she didn't at least try to find the answers.

An idea that might persuade Jarrod to help her popped into her head. "What if Jasper already talked to Thomas? Maybe that's why he said 'K. C.'"

Jarrod sucked in his bottom lip, holding her gaze as if searching for something deep within her. Was he disappointed that she wanted to pursue this thread? Did he think she was heartless?

"We don't know that he said 'K. C.,' remember?" he said at last. "Olivia said 'Casey.' Subtle difference."

"There's only one way to find out," Isabelle challenged.

Jarrod scrutinized her for several long seconds, but she didn't back down. They could call every Michelle Blacke on their list and not learn anything. Meanwhile, Thomas Reid was on this island.

"I'll talk to Thomas," Jarrod finally said. "He might be more willing to listen to someone he knows rather than a complete stranger."

"Who might be his sister."

"Or who might be crazy." His sudden grin softened his words. "Think of it from his perspective. Most people don't get calls from someone claiming to be a long-lost relative."

True. But Isabelle had never expected to be searching for a possible brother either. Or having to contemplate what his existence meant when it came to the esteem she'd always held for her father. Davis Byrnes had been an upstanding man, respected by all who knew him. A loving husband, a doting father. How could such an honorable, trustworthy person hide a second family?

The birth certificates had made a chink in her father's armor, one that Isabelle desperately wanted to repair. But what if talking to Thomas widened that chink? She had to take that risk to learn the truth about her father and about her own place in the Byrnes family tree.

Isabelle waited on pins and needles as Jarrod entered Thomas's number into his phone. The tension climbed when the call went to voice mail.

"Hey, Thomas, this is Jarrod Long. Call me when you get a chance. It's important." He disconnected and faced Isabelle. "Nothing to do now except wait for him to call back. Patiently."

"Patience is usually considered one of my virtues. But it's hard to wait when the answer seems so close."

"Waiting is usually hard, no matter the circumstances," Jarrod said softly.

A twinge of guilt squeezed Isabelle's heart. How could she be annoyed about waiting for a return phone call when Jarrod desperately needed good news about his brother? She wasn't that heartless, was she?

No. She was simply frightened by the events of the last couple of days and eager to know the truth about her family. And hopeful that Thomas Reid could provide that truth. But until Jarrod talked to him, all she could do was wait.

Isabelle walked to the window and gazed out at the bending branches of the nearby palm trees. "The rain has let up. I should return to the hotel before it starts storming again. Heather is probably bored out of her mind."

"She needs you to entertain her?"

"When no one else is available."

Jarrod slowly rose from the chair. "I'll drive you."

"Are we going to have this argument again?" Isabelle tried to keep her tone light, but she didn't quite succeed. "I'll call a cab."

"I'll drop you off at the hotel, then go back to the hospital," Jarrod offered.

"The hotel isn't on your way. You'll be crossing that bridge twice."

"Okay. Take a cab, and I'll follow it."

Isabelle threw up her hands in surrender and immediately regretted the gesture. She probably needed another pain pill and a long nap.

Neither of them said much during the drive. Most of the debris from the accident had been cleared from the bridge, but only one lane was open, which caused a delay. Isabelle shut her eyes until they were past the horrific scene.

Jarrod parked near the hotel's entrance, then hopped out and hurried around to the passenger side.

Isabelle was fully capable of opening her own car door, but the chivalrous gesture warmed her heart—a heart that was drawn to this man in ways she didn't understand and wasn't sure she should explore. Though she wanted to, she admitted to herself. Very much.

They walked together into the lobby.

As they approached the elevators, Jarrod touched her arm. "Would you like to have dinner with me this evening?"

His voice was so low that Isabelle wasn't sure she'd heard him correctly. But the question danced in her mind before settling in a quiet place deep inside her. At this moment, Jarrod wasn't a security expert asking his client to join him for an evening meal. He was a man—a man she was deeply attracted to despite her attempts not to be—asking her on a date.

Of that she had no doubt.

Neither could she doubt her answer.

It went beyond all sense, and she prided herself on being sensible. She was, after all, more comfortable in dusty archives and arcane databases than interacting with the social conventions that Heather coveted so much and scrabbled so hard to achieve.

Why was life so often that way, where the grass seemed greener on the other side of the hedge?

"I'd enjoy that," Isabelle whispered.

The quietest sigh passed his lips, as if he'd been holding his breath while awaiting her answer, and his chin dipped slightly. "Do you like seafood? There's a place near here that has the best hush puppies you've ever tasted."

She grinned. "Don't be so sure about that. I'm a hush puppy connoisseur."

"Just wait and see." Jarrod smiled. "Is seven o'clock too early?"

"Seven is fine."

Despite her body's aches and the emotional stress of the past couple of days, Isabelle's spirit danced as the elevator carried her up to her suite.

The dancing ended as she prepared to knock on the door. Heather waited inside, either peeved at being shut in her room most of the day or overly eager to hear all the juicy details of Isabelle's accident so she could relay an exaggerated version to her friends. She definitely wouldn't be pleased to learn Isabelle had dinner plans for the evening.

Isabelle straightened her shoulders as her stomach knotted into a tangled mass. "Why, oh, why," she murmured, "couldn't you have stayed home, Heather?"

Isabelle folded her arms and wished she had remained at the safe house instead of returning to the hotel. Though Heather had told Isabelle she planned to stay in all day, she'd braved the storm to go shopping. She spent the first half hour of Isabelle's return complaining about the stores, the salesclerks, the lack of fashion in the shops, and the incompetence of the hotel bellman who'd fumbled with her shopping bags.

Heather didn't take a breath during her harangue, nor did she ask Isabelle about the accident. The event appeared to be totally blocked from her stepmother's mind.

The onslaught of words pressed against Isabelle's skull and tightened her shoulders, reawakening the aches caused by her instinct to stiffen her muscles before she rear-ended the vehicle in front of her.

When Heather finally calmed down, Isabelle excused herself to take a hot soak in the luxurious spa tub.

She emerged an hour later, relaxed and refreshed, and joined Heather at the round table in front of the giant window.

Heather was playing solitaire on her tablet. She had a strange affinity for the game, which didn't fit with the high-society persona she took such pains to cultivate. Heather even prided herself on having never lost a game, even when she re-dealt a few times to achieve that win. If she didn't meet her goal on the first try, she changed the variables until she was victorious.

"I thought we could order room service for dinner." Heather focused on her screen as she talked, barely acknowledging Isabelle's presence. "Or have something delivered from one of the nearby restaurants. Perhaps find a good murder mystery to watch. A scary whodunit seems appropriate for this weather."

"I already have plans," Isabelle said quietly.

Heather glanced up. "What plans?"

"Jarrod asked me to dinner."

"Who's Jarrod?" Heather demanded shrilly.

"His brother is the private investigator who was shot," Isabelle explained. "Now Jarrod is helping me."

Her stepmother gave a haughty sniff. "Professionals don't mix business with pleasure. I suppose he knows how rich you are."

"We haven't discussed our finances." Isabelle's voice was harsher than she intended. Once again, she found herself wishing her stepmother had stayed home.

"What am I supposed to do?" Heather whined. "Sit here by myself?"

Unspoken words hung between them, but Isabelle refused to fall for Heather's obvious expectation of an invitation to join them.

"If you wish," Isabelle said. The anguished look on Heather's face, whether genuine or feigned, shot an arrow of guilt into her conscience. She softened her tone. "I shouldn't be out too late. We can watch a movie when I get back."

"Great." Heather moved from the table and plopped down in the middle of the white sofa. "Some girls' trip this is turning out to be."

Isabelle slipped back into her room, tamping down all the words she wanted to spew at her stepmother, words she'd kept inside for years to keep the peace between them. She'd never wanted her dad to feel the need to step in as referee or to choose his daughter over his wife. Or vice versa—a scenario that would have left a permanent wound in Isabelle's heart. But as she opened the bedroom door, something snapped inside her. Dad was gone, and Heather was an uninvited guest on this trip.

She whirled around to find Heather staring at her with an expression that Isabelle had never seen before. Anger? Hatred?

Heather blinked, and the odd expression disappeared. Now she resembled a sulking child, unhappy she wasn't getting her way.

"This was never supposed to be a girls' trip," Isabelle said, struggling to keep her frustration in check. "It was *my* trip. And so far, it hasn't been much fun. Someone almost shot me. My laptop and files have been stolen. And I caused a multicar wreck on the bridge."

Heather opened her mouth to speak.

Isabelle raised a hand to stop her. "A nice man asked me to dinner. He has been the only one to show me the kind of compassion Dad would have shown me." She averted her eyes and took a deep breath, then stared at Heather again. "You've shown me nothing."

Before Heather could respond, Isabelle stepped into her room and quietly shut the door behind her. Her chest heaved, and she covered her mouth, shock washing over her at the stand she'd taken. She was practically giddy with a strange sense of relief but also weighed down by guilt.

What would her dad think if he'd witnessed that scene? Upset that she'd talked to Heather that way? Or proud that she'd stood up for herself?

If the confrontation had been with anyone but Heather, Isabelle would know the answer. If this moment had happened before she found the birth certificates, she might have made a good guess.

But the father she thought she knew so well had kept a huge secret from her. For the first time, she realized her anger at Heather might be directed at the wrong person.

How could Isabelle possibly release the stony anger that pressed against her chest toward the one person she loved most in this world? Especially now that he was gone?

But the anger was there, pulsating like a living thing, fed by the knowledge that her father hadn't trusted her with the most important details of her life.

The upscale seafood restaurant was everything Jarrod had promised and more. Heavy rain pounded the windows that ran along the
length of the dining area, but Isabelle felt that the storm added to the
cozy atmosphere of their corner table. Hurricane lamps were spaced
at intervals along the walls and provided romantic ambient lighting.

Nautical themes were overdone to the point of cliché in seafood
restaurants up and down the Atlantic coast, but this venue's marine
decor—with its antique buoys, a figurehead recovered from a sunken
ship, and used netting—had achieved a refreshing authenticity. The
lanterns decorating the polished wood tables appeared to have been
salvaged from antique stores and thrift shops, then gently refurbished
so that no two were alike.

In the dimness, Isabelle could imagine Jarrod as a long-ago sea
captain. He even wore a dusky blue fisherman sweater, which emphasized
his athletic build, over pressed khakis. To avoid staring at him and to
calm her fluttering heart, she focused on her menu and munched on
one of the hush puppies the waiter had delivered when seating them.
She had to admit that they were top-notch.

Once their orders were taken, Jarrod gave her an awkward smile.
"I heard from Thomas. He'll meet us at my office tomorrow morning."

A surge of excitement raced up her spine. This was the best
news she'd had since she started her quest. Isabelle had wanted to
ask about Thomas as soon as Jarrod stepped into the hotel lobby
and found her waiting for him, but she feared that if he didn't have

any news, her disappointment would ruin their dinner. "What did you tell him?"

"That someone asked me to make an introduction." The gold flecks in Jarrod's eyes glowed. "I didn't want him doing an Internet search on you."

"I imagine that's something you've already done," she said.

"Guilty." He looked sheepish at his admission. "It's something I would have done with anyone under these circumstances."

"It's okay." Isabelle grinned. "I did a search on you too."

"Color me surprised." Jarrod chuckled. "Find out anything interesting?"

"Nothing beyond what's on your website." She tilted her head. "Absolutely nothing on social media. Very odd in this day and age."

"Not for those in my line of work. But you?" Jarrod slowly shook his head, and his smile widened. "A website for your company. Social media posts and photos. I know the books you've read and the movies you've seen. I found out that you love to cook, but your attempts at baking almost always end in disaster."

Isabelle's cheeks flushed, but she didn't try to hide her embarrassment. "You must have seen the photo of my three-tiered German chocolate cake."

He laughed. "And your ruined apple pie and rock-hard snickerdoodles."

Isabelle laughed with him. "At least I try," she said with a self-conscious shrug.

"That's one of the things I like about you."

One of the things? What else does he like about me? The lantern's soft lighting seemed to cast an aura around them, shielding them from anyone else in the room, as his words settled into her heart.

"You're not afraid to share your failures," Jarrod continued.

"Only those in the kitchen," Isabelle admitted. To overcome her sudden awkwardness, she snagged another hush puppy. "You were right about these. What's their secret?"

"Even with all my investigative skills, I've never been able to find out. That recipe is heavily guarded."

Their small talk continued until the waiter brought their entrées, grilled sea bass with orange-ginger glaze for Isabelle and pan-seared salmon served with scallops and macadamia-cilantro pesto for Jarrod. The food was delicious.

While enjoying their meal, they both abided by a silent agreement to pretend they were two ordinary people out on a casual date instead of strangers who'd been thrown together by circumstances neither of them understood.

During the drive to the restaurant, Jarrod had told Isabelle that Jasper's vital signs were improving and doctors were cautiously optimistic regarding his prognosis. Over dessert of mini cheesecakes with wine gelées, he shared hilarious anecdotes from his childhood. Though Jarrod and Jasper were six years apart in age, they'd gotten into a few scrapes together.

After one particularly funny story, which Isabelle assumed was 90 percent true and 10 percent exaggeration, she laughed until she cried, then patted her face with her napkin. The last thing she wanted was mascara running down her cheeks.

"Jasper and I spent some time together before the shooting," she said. "We share an interest in Florida's unique history. I'm very sorry he was shot because of me."

"He was doing his job," Jarrod said quietly. "I know my brother better than anyone. I have no doubt he'd do what he did all over again if he were given the option."

No matter what he said, Isabelle could never wish anyone to go through such a horrific experience for her. "Jasper is in my prayers." She raised her gaze to Jarrod's. "His whole family is."

His expression softened with surprise. "Including me?"

"Including you." Isabelle's cheeks heated, but she didn't look away. Something was happening between them. She didn't understand it. She doubted Jarrod did either. But he must recognize, as she did, the growing attraction between them.

"Thank you." Jarrod extended his hand toward her.

After a short pause, she slipped her hand into his. Her skin tingled while butterflies danced in her stomach.

They lingered a little longer over their dessert. Isabelle didn't want the night to end.

When they returned to Isabelle's hotel, Jarrod walked her inside.

Isabelle scanned the lobby, expecting to find Heather lounging in one of the seating areas. Other guests were grouped here and there, but she didn't see Heather among them. The weight in Isabelle's stomach, a weight she hadn't even realized was there until that moment, dissipated.

"How about a cup of coffee?" Jarrod motioned toward the café.

Isabelle hesitated, unsure how to respond. On one hand, she still felt bad for how she'd left things with Heather.

On the other hand, Isabelle wasn't ready for the date to end. Still buoyed by the news that she'd meet Thomas tomorrow, she wasn't anxious to face Heather, who was sure to pop Isabelle's imaginary balloon with her sulkiness, wittingly or not.

Even if Heather had gotten over her snit, she'd certainly ask all kinds of impertinent questions about Isabelle's dinner date and follow those up with snarky comments. If Isabelle said she'd ordered the sea bass, Heather would want to know why she hadn't gone with the lobster. She'd disparage the choice of dessert and the choice of anything else she could come up with.

Better to put off all that negativity as long as possible.

"I'd love to," Isabelle said. "As long as I can get a ginger ale. Coffee will keep me up too late."

"Two ginger ales then." Jarrod held out his arm, then escorted her to the table.

Isabelle felt the eyes of other guests on them as they strolled through the lobby. Ladies cast admiring glances toward Jarrod. And maybe even one or two appreciative glimpses came her way from the gentlemen.

Isabelle tightened her grip on Jarrod's arm before she realized what she was doing, as if she were signaling, *He's mine, ladies.* That was absurd.

Jarrod gave her a pleased smile and covered her hand with his. Perhaps he was sending a loud and clear signal of his own.

Isabelle hoped so, then inwardly chided herself for making such a to-do over a simple gesture. It wasn't like they were engaged or even dating. In a few days, she'd return home. When that happened, she'd probably never see Jarrod again.

But that didn't mean she couldn't enjoy her time with him while it lasted.

When the waiter brought their glasses of ginger ale, he handed a plastic pouch to Jarrod and murmured something to him before strolling away.

Jarrod's smile dissolved.

Isabelle braced herself. She intuitively sensed that the pleasantness of the evening was about to end. "Maybe I should have ordered something stronger."

"Maybe."

"What is it?"

He didn't answer as he scanned the room.

A knot caught in her throat. "It must be bad."

Jarrod took her hand.

His touch was warm and comforting, strong and safe. But were all these feelings only an illusion? She wouldn't even know this man if the detective she'd hired hadn't been shot. And now it was as if she depended on Jarrod for her very life. Any feelings stirred by his touch couldn't be real. Could they?

"I don't like giving this to you, but I can't hide it either." He set the pouch on the table. "The valet found this on my windshield. The waiter gave it to me with our order."

Isabelle's stomach clenched as she regarded the pouch. "What's in it?"

"Black petals."

After the introductions were made, Jarrod invited Isabelle and the Reids to take seats in his office. The upholstered chairs surrounded a square coffee table and provided a more intimate setting than a conference room. Jarrod wanted everyone to feel as comfortable as possible. An assistant delivered steaming cups of coffee, then left, discreetly closing the door behind her.

K. C. Reid eyed Isabelle as she sipped from her cup, no doubt taking in the expensive cut of Isabelle's clothing.

Until that moment, Jarrod hadn't considered the possibility that the Reids might have surmised that the meeting had something to do with K. C.'s campaign for the Florida House of Representatives. K. C. was clearly and eagerly calculating how large a campaign donation she could wring from Isabelle. And perhaps wondering what Isabelle, the epitome of an upper-class, highly educated young woman who lived outside the district, would want in exchange for her support.

Jarrod had to give K. C. credit. She obviously didn't plan to be the first one to bring up the campaign

"Jarrod tells me you've lived here most of your life," Isabelle said to Thomas. "I haven't been able to see much of the island because of the rain. But it must be a lovely place."

"It's home," Thomas replied warmly.

Jarrod wondered if Thomas was surprised that Isabelle was directing the conversation to him instead of K. C.

"My family settled here after World War II," Thomas continued. "Apparently, my grandfather did his training at Camp Blanding near Jacksonville. When the war ended, he traveled around Florida and finally settled here."

"I've often heard variations of that story as I talk to people about their family trees," Isabelle said. Jarrod had told the Reids that she was a genealogist when he introduced her. "The soldiers must have been impressed by Florida's exotic beauty. My family moved here from Charleston, South Carolina, in the 1890s."

"Genealogical research must be fascinating," K. C. said, practically purring.

At least that was how she sounded to Jarrod. He didn't know why he disliked her. Maybe it was because he rarely trusted a politician, including the ones who paid his company the big bucks for his services.

"I enjoy the work very much," Isabelle said. "In fact, that's why I'm here."

K. C.'s expression turned from simpering to enthusiastic in a heartbeat. "If you're in the market for a client, I'm your gal. I've always wanted to explore my family's tree. A distant cousin worked on it once several years ago when that was all the rage. But I'm sure she didn't know what she was doing. It would be so much better to have the research done by a professional."

"Isabelle isn't here to research your family tree," Jarrod told K. C., keeping his tone cordial.

Not that it mattered. Once again, K. C.'s demeanor changed. Now she appeared insulted, but that persona also quickly transformed into candidate mode. *She must have remembered that Isabelle might be interested in donating to her campaign.*

"Then why are you here?" K. C. asked brightly. "Are you planning to move to the island? If so, we'd be happy to help you find the perfect home. Thomas is a successful real estate agent. And I'd be honored to introduce you to the crème de la crème of our local population. We may not be as genteel here on our little island as you're used to, but we have a marvelous time in our social circle."

"Thank you," Isabelle said graciously. "But I have no intention of leaving my home. I'm here for a completely different reason."

"I see." K. C.'s avaricious look deepened.

Or maybe Jarrod was simply seeing what he wanted to see. He expected K. C. to be greedy, so greed was what he saw. He might go along with that if he were a regular joe. But he'd had enough training in reading people's body language to know his impression of K. C. was accurate and not influenced by his own perceptions. She was hoping for a big donation from the cultured young woman sitting near her.

And she was about to be extremely disappointed.

Jarrod cleared his throat and addressed Thomas. "Isabelle has something to ask you. It may be a difficult question for you to hear."

Thomas stared at Isabelle, his eyes wide with curiosity and concern. "What is it?"

"I don't know how to ask this except to just ask it," Isabelle said. "Is there any chance you could be adopted?"

"Adopted?" The word exploded from K. C.'s lips. "Why would you think such a thing?"

Isabelle glanced at K. C., then returned her focus to Thomas. Her hands were neatly folded in her lap as she waited for his answer. She came across as calm, cool, and collected, but from his vantage point, Jarrod could see that her knuckles were white.

Thomas, on the other hand, seemed to be undergoing a transformation. Jarrod could almost sense the thoughts whirling in his mind as he considered how to answer Isabelle's question. After a moment, his shoulders, which had tensed at first, relaxed, and he gave Isabelle a shy smile. "Honestly? I've often wondered."

K. C. started to bluster something incoherent.

But Isabelle's calm voice quieted her. "Why did you wonder?"

"I don't resemble my parents. Not in the slightest." Thomas rested his ankle on the opposite knee, his body language open and honest. "I even asked once when I was in high school. Mom said that was a silly notion, but she didn't exactly deny it. I could tell she was upset, so I never brought it up again."

"You think you're adopted?" K. C.'s strident voice filled the room. "That's nonsense. There would be records."

"I might have those," Isabelle said. "At least I did."

"What is that supposed to mean?" K. C. snapped.

She didn't act as friendly now that she knew Isabelle wasn't a potential campaign donor. Perhaps this revelation was too much for her. She had a sense of who she was, who her family was—the picture-perfect image shared on billboards, social media, and television commercials. Isabelle was about to change all that. Though that wasn't necessarily a bad thing. K. C. could do a lot worse than to have it known around town that her husband was a Byrnes.

Isabelle described how she'd discovered the birth certificates in her late father's safe and her subsequent search for Michelle Blacke. "I believe you're Michelle's son. Maybe my father's son. There's one way to be sure, if you're willing."

"You want me to take a DNA test," Thomas finished for her.

Jarrod had to hand it to the man—he was taking the news like a champ. Or maybe like someone who had always expected this. His mother might not have wanted to tell him the truth, but somewhere in the world was someone else who might. And that person had suddenly arrived.

"Would you?" Isabelle asked.

"We'll have to think about it." K. C. stood and slung the strap of her bag over her shoulder. "We need to go. This has been quite an unexpected development, and we both need time to process it."

Thomas shrugged and rose from his chair. "It's been a pleasure meeting you, Isabelle. We'll talk again soon."

"Thank you," Isabelle said as she stood. "I look forward to it."

Jarrod got up and stood next to Isabelle.

K. C. tugged on Thomas's arm as if she couldn't get out of the office fast enough.

"I'll call you," Thomas said to Jarrod.

K. C. pulled her husband through the door.

Once they were gone, Jarrod remarked, "That went well."

"Did it?"

"Thomas is too curious not to follow up. And so is K. C."

"Then why did she drag him out of here?" Isabelle asked. "You would have thought the poor man was headed for an execution."

"It wasn't that bad." Jarrod chuckled. "Remember that K. C. is running for a major office. She probably wants to talk to her campaign manager before deciding what to do. Try to figure out how this kind of news might affect her election."

"Why would voters care?"

"They probably won't, but K. C. will want to be sure of that." He gave Isabelle an encouraging smile. "I'm starving. How about I treat you to lunch?"

"My turn to treat," Isabelle said firmly. "But you'll need to choose the place since you know the best local spots."

"Then I choose—" Jarrod's phone vibrated, and he checked the screen. "It's my mechanic friend. This could be about your car."

Isabelle watched Jarrod during his brief conversation with the mechanic. From his expression, the news wasn't good. The pebble that had settled in her stomach during the Reids' abrupt departure grew into a heavy stone.

"What did he say?" she asked as soon as Jarrod ended the call.

"The accident wasn't your fault." He took her hands in his. "Someone tampered with your brakes."

Isabelle gasped and tightened her grip on Jarrod's hands. She knew he was trying to make her feel better when he said the accident wasn't her fault, that he wanted her to let go of the guilt she'd carried since she'd slammed into the first car. But no matter why the brakes went out, she was still to blame. Someone wanted her to be injured—maybe even killed—and didn't care if innocent people got caught up in it. Who could want her out of the way that badly? And why?

Isabelle withdrew her hand and hugged her body as an uncontrollable trembling seized her. "What do I do?" She barely croaked the question.

Jarrod pulled her into a gentle embrace. "I'm not going to let anyone hurt you."

"You can't be with me 24-7."

"Who says I can't?"

Isabelle appreciated the protection he offered her, but she felt cowardly, as if she weren't brave or strong enough to protect herself. No modern heroine was supposed to need a man to save her from her enemies. But Isabelle wasn't a heroine or an action figure. She could put on a brave front, but her insides felt like melted cheese.

"I'll hire you to find out who did this," she said. "I mean, your firm. That way I won't be imposing on your kindness."

"It's not kindness. It's—" Jarrod abruptly stopped talking as words seemed to fail him.

Isabelle couldn't guess what he refrained from saying. Maybe he didn't know himself. "I just wish I understood why this was happening."

"So do I."

"I should go back to the hotel. Stay there with Heather in case whoever is doing this decides to go after her."

"Has she received any threats?" Jarrod asked. "Any black tulips?"

"None that I know of. I'm sure she would tell me if she did." In fact, Heather was probably miffed to be excluded as a victim of the anonymous warnings. Isabelle could already picture the woman's hysterical sobs and clutching fingers grabbing Jarrod or one of his guards. Heather would definitely revel in the experience of being guarded by a private security force because of the threat against Isabelle. She'd have a wonderful new story to tell her society friends—one that few, if any, of them could top.

"I'll contact Captain Palmer and give him an update. He needs to know about this." Jarrod stepped away to make the call.

Isabelle shivered. Someone had tampered with her brakes, causing a multicar pileup on a long bridge during a horrific storm.

Who hated her enough to do something like that?

Isabelle pulled Heather's Audi into the drive of the neat bungalow. Her stepmother had been furious to learn that Isabelle had met Thomas Reid and his wife without her. Though Isabelle was certain that if Heather had had her way, the meeting wouldn't have taken place at all, which was exactly why Isabelle hadn't told her ahead of time.

Now she regretted telling her afterward.

Jarrod had insisted on accompanying Isabelle to the suite after driving her back to the hotel. But Isabelle insisted he leave once they reached her door. She anticipated Heather's disappointment at being excluded from the meeting. With Jarrod as her audience, Heather's histrionics might never end.

Isabelle could understand disappointment and self-pity. That was Heather's modus operandi. But she'd been stunned by the ferocious anger Heather hurled at her, as if the meeting was an unforgivable betrayal. After slinging her vindictive insults, Heather stormed out of the suite, leaving Isabelle curled in a corner of the couch, flooded with self-doubt and loneliness.

Until Thomas texted her with an invitation to join him at his parents' home.

Heather's car fob rested in a bowl on the console table near the suite's entryway, so she might have gone to the hotel's café. Before Isabelle could talk herself out of the impulse, she'd scribbled a hasty note, then took the stairs to the parking garage. She wanted to avoid Heather, and she also suspected either Jarrod or one of his security team had the hotel under surveillance. Isabelle didn't want anyone following her.

Now Isabelle sat in the elder Reids' driveway, rain streaming down the windows, doubting the wisdom of her impulsive behavior. She was on this quest for answers because of a similar impulse, and all she had to show for it was one catastrophe after another. When had she become someone who acted on a whim instead of thoughtfully considering all the angles before taking action? Had her detailed, cautious temperament been upended by her grief?

More likely, it had been upended by the unexpected discovery of the birth certificates.

Isabelle rested her forehead on the steering wheel. Her neck and shoulder muscles, still aching from the accident, tightened from the stress. Heather's erratic rant echoed in her ears as the storm pounded against the car.

Her gloomy thoughts were distracted by a rap against the glass.

Thomas stood beside the driver's door beneath a green golf umbrella. He gave her a cautious smile.

Isabelle responded with a weak smile of her own and unlocked the door.

The events she'd set into motion by suggesting a DNA test had taken on a life of their own. What happened after she stepped out of this vehicle was out of her control. She'd rushed here at Thomas's request because she needed answers. But what could she say to Thomas and his parents? Would Jack and Linda Reid consider her a monster for suggesting to their son he'd been adopted—a secret they might have hidden from him for his entire life? Or did they hope to convince her that she was wrong? Maybe she was. But a sidelong glance at the younger version of her father beside her said otherwise.

Though rain still fell, the sheets slanted by the brisk tropical winds, sunshine pushed through the gray clouds. It was a quirk of Florida that Isabelle loved. And at this moment, the beam of light cutting through the dark storm seemed like a ray of hope sent from God.

She exited the car, and Thomas gripped her elbow while holding the umbrella over both of them. Together they hurried to the shelter of the porch.

"Thanks for coming." Thomas shook excess water from the umbrella and set it in a corner. "This is probably awkward for you."

"For you too, I imagine."

"It's time for the secrets to be told." His confident tone belied the uncertainty reflected in his eyes. "I'm not sure why they didn't tell me when I was a kid."

"So it's true?" Isabelle asked. "You *are* adopted?"

The genuine warmth of his smile eased the tension in her muscles. "Come inside. My parents are anxious to meet you."

Isabelle squared her shoulders and preceded Thomas into the house.

Jack and Linda stood in the foyer, wearing pinched smiles. Isabelle couldn't blame them. This couldn't be a pleasant situation for them.

Once the introductions and greetings were said, Linda suggested they gather around the dining room table. It was set with a tea service, dessert plates, and a covered cake platter. Family photographs and shadow boxes with various mementos graced the room's golden walls. A brass chandelier centered above the table provided light.

Thomas pulled a chair out for Isabelle and took a seat beside her.

Linda served scrumptious slices of red velvet cake with buttercream icing, and Jack poured cups of cinnamon-scented tea.

"Where's K. C.?" Isabelle asked.

"We came here after meeting with you and Jarrod," Thomas answered. "K. C. didn't take the news very well when Mom and Dad . . ." He stared down at his plate as if fumbling to find the right words.

Isabelle's heart ached for him. She'd never meant to cause disruption to a family, but that was what her quest for the truth had done.

Linda placed a comforting hand on Thomas's arm. She regarded Isabelle with a firm yet sympathetic gaze. "Jack and I finally did what we should have done a long time ago. It's true that Thomas is adopted, but honestly, he's been ours as much as any biological child could be. He's our son, and the legalities have never been anything we dwelled on too much. It was so easy to let the days slip by without talking about the past."

"Anyway," Thomas said, squeezing his mother's hand, "when I said I was inviting you here to talk to Mom and Dad, K. C. left. I suppose she needs more time to process the news. It's a very startling thing to grasp."

"You're right." Isabelle wrapped her fingers around the porcelain teacup, letting its warmth flow through her while she searched for what to say. All she could do was speak the truth. "It's difficult to grow up believing one thing only to find out you may have been mistaken."

"That's the part of the story I don't understand," Jack said. "Are you adopted too?"

"I'm not sure," Isabelle admitted.

"I told them about the birth certificates," Thomas said. "But they'd like to hear the story from you if you don't mind telling it again."

Isabelle obliged, once again sharing the strange saga.

When she finished, Jack set down his cup. "Just so we understand, you believe that you and Thomas are siblings?"

"Possibly. Or maybe he's my half brother." Isabelle shrugged. "I don't know."

"There is a slight resemblance," Linda said. "I suppose you could be related."

Isabelle and Thomas exchanged embarrassed glances, as if they wanted to search the other's face to find any connection between them but also didn't want to stare. Yet it was there when they smiled—the single dimple.

"I always wanted a sister," Thomas said with a self-conscious laugh. "I even asked Santa Claus for one a couple of times."

"That he did," Linda agreed. She seemed to be far away, lost in the memory of long-ago Christmases.

"Never a brother?" Isabelle teased.

"I'm not sure my motives were all that pure." Thomas laughed again, this time with more ease. "I thought I could boss a little sister around, but a brother might try to boss me around. That's how it worked in my friends' families."

Isabelle smiled, but deep inside she felt a pang of sorrow for the bossing around she might have missed out on because she and Thomas—if he was indeed her brother—had been adopted by different families. She studied the Reids' home. It was spacious and cozy, though much smaller than the Byrnes' mansion. What would it have been like to have grown up here, with this couple as her parents instead of the ones she'd known?

For a brief second, she wished she could have lived a parallel life, one in each place so she could experience what she had missed yet retain what she'd had. Her emotions were a tangled mess as the longing for both pasts pierced her heart.

With Isabelle's encouragement, Thomas shared more about his childhood while they finished their cake and tea.

When the dishes were cleared away, the mood shifted from the gaiety they'd been experiencing to something more sober. Linda placed a folder on the table between them.

Beneath the table, Isabelle clenched her hands. This was the moment. What would Linda reveal?

"We know nothing about Thomas's birth parents," she said. "The adoption was a closed one."

"What exactly do you mean by that?" Isabelle asked, her voice trembling.

Jack cleared his throat before answering. "There was a go-between. An attorney. He assured us everything was aboveboard, but the birth family insisted on complete discretion and secrecy. All the expenses were paid for by a private benefactor. All we had to do was raise Thomas as our own."

Isabelle clenched her hands tighter. "You have no idea who this benefactor was?"

"We didn't." Jack sighed heavily as he pulled his phone from a pocket. "But after K. C. left, I did an online search for your name. No offense, but I wanted to be sure you were legitimate before we invited you into our home."

"I understand," Isabelle assured him. "These are uncharted waters for all of us."

Jack focused on his phone, tapping the screen, then held it out for Isabelle to see. "Is this your father?"

The photo was from her website, and it showed Dad standing beside her while she proudly displayed her college diploma. "Yes."

"He was there," Linda said.

Taken aback by the simple declaration, Isabelle furrowed her brow. "Where?"

"When we were given Thomas," Linda replied.

"He was much younger, of course," Jack added. "But it was definitely him."

Isabelle leaned back in her chair, as if the news were a giant hand pressing against her chest. Even though she'd speculated that her father was involved in the adoptions—he must have been, since he had the birth certificates—she hadn't prepared herself for receiving confirmation on that front. "You mean he was the attorney."

The question came out more like a statement, as if she needed that to be the role he'd played. Though she knew it wasn't true. The more time she spent with Thomas, the more he reminded her of Dad. It was more than the shape of his nose and the set and color of his eyes. The left corner of his mouth quirked when he smiled, just like Dad's. He tended to rub his thumb along his jawline, an unconscious gesture, just like Dad. Even his speech seemed to have the same cadence. Her heart pinched, the similarities both deepening and easing her grief.

"No, he wasn't the attorney," Jack said. "I always assumed he was our mysterious benefactor."

"He stayed outside," Linda rushed to explain. "We happened to see the car pull up and the attorney get out of the driver's seat." She pointed to the photo on Jack's phone. "He exited on the passenger side and pulled Thomas's car seat from the back. I don't think they knew we were watching."

"Then someone from the adoption agency escorted us to a meeting room," Jack said, picking up the threads of the story. "The attorney came in alone, carrying Thomas. We signed a few papers, and we took our baby home."

Linda gave a strange laugh. "I remember thinking how simple it was. After all our waiting and hoping, within five minutes we were a family. It scared me how quick and easy it was." She laughed again, a nervous giggle this time. "I don't think I slept a wink that first month—and not because Thomas kept me up. I simply couldn't believe he was ours, that there hadn't been some mistake. I was sure there was a catch somewhere and the attorney would come back and take him away again."

"I saw the man I assumed was our benefactor a few other times over the years," Jack admitted. "Once when I was coaching Thomas's soccer team, he was standing by the bleachers. I tried to find him after the game, but he must have already left."

"And that time Thomas was in the hospital," Linda said. "His appendix ruptured, and we were there several days. I'm sure I saw him a couple of times then too."

"It sounds like he was watching out for you," Isabelle said to Thomas.

He nodded. "My secret guardian angel. I'm sorry I never got to thank him."

"Is it possible," Linda began, then stopped to wipe a tear from her cheek. "Could he be Thomas's father?"

"I don't know." Isabelle wasn't ready to tell these people that she and Thomas might have shared a father, not without concrete evidence. On some level, she still believed there might be another explanation.

"Because of the name on the birth certificates?" Thomas asked.

"I met a woman at Jasper Long's detective agency who bears an eerie resemblance to me," Isabelle explained. "She said her name was Morgan Young. But I think she may be Michelle Blacke. I believe she's our mom."

Thomas sucked in a sharp breath and opened his mouth as if to speak, then closed it again.

"You remind me so much of Dad," Isabelle told Thomas. Then a different idea popped into her mind—one that could explain how Thomas resembled her father so strongly but exonerated Davis from suspicions of an extramarital affair. "I wonder if he's Michelle Blacke's brother."

As soon as the words were out of her mouth, she sat back in surprise. How could that be? According to the Byrnes' genealogical records, Davis was an only child. Her heart sank, but it was too late to quell the horrid thought. Had someone altered the information? Impossible. But what if it were true?

"You think Davis found a family for me," Thomas said. His gaze darted to his parents, then landed on Isabelle. "And then, when another baby came along, he and his wife adopted you."

"Maybe," Isabelle said as hot tears burned. Whether or not Michelle was Davis's sister, Isabelle acknowledged what her heart knew to be true. "We're siblings, Thomas. You know it as well as I do. We need to prove it."

Once they did, maybe the bearer of the black tulip petals would stop leaving threatening notes. If the truth of the relationship was what that person hoped to prevent.

If not, Isabelle might spend the rest of her days looking over her shoulder.

Jarrod privately vowed to himself that if Heather, whom he'd immediately recognized from the photos Samantha had sent him the day before, rolled her eyes or said the word *unfair* one more time, he'd walk out of the hotel café and never return. He'd been intrigued by Isabelle's call asking him to meet her and Thomas. And more than a little miffed to find out Isabelle had snuck out of the hotel under Dax's nose to meet with Thomas and his parents.

As much as he hated to admit it, he also understood why Thomas felt obligated to include his wife in the impromptu meeting. But instead of getting down to business, Heather was holding all of them captive with her self-centered complaints.

From what Jarrod had managed to decipher from their disjointed conversation, Isabelle had left the hotel without telling her stepmother—she'd even taken her car—and when Heather read the note that Isabelle had left, she parked herself in the hotel garage to wait for Isabelle's return.

He wished he'd had time to talk to Isabelle in private before the five of them settled in the quiet corner table at the café. That lack bothered him more than it should—more than he wanted it to. A few days ago, he hadn't even known she existed. Now, thoughts of her filled his every waking moment.

Jarrod admitted that Isabelle didn't consume his thoughts because she was a client or because she might know something that would help him find who had tried to kill Jasper. His care for her went deeper than both those considerations. And that wasn't a good thing. Not when he had multiple mysteries to solve and needed all his senses on high alert.

Staying away from Isabelle didn't make her any less of a distraction. In fact, that made the situation even worse. At least when she was with him, he knew she was safe. That he could protect her from whoever had shot Jasper and trashed his office, from whoever was leaving the black tulip petals and anonymous notes.

"I don't see how you can be so certain," Heather told Isabelle for the umpteenth time. "All you have are conjectures and vain hopes. Baby Girl Blacke may have the same birth date as you, but that doesn't mean you're her, especially since you have a legal birth certificate of your own. And I'm sure your father would have told me if he had a son or a nephew hidden away somewhere. He told me everything."

Jarrod glanced at Isabelle, concerned about the effect of Heather's strident words.

Isabelle's arms were folded across her chest, her lips pressed together, her shoulders taut. She didn't say a word, but her body language clearly screamed, *Don't be so sure about that.*

At least there wasn't anyone seated near enough to them to overhear the strange conversation.

"I warned you about this," Heather said, pointing at Isabelle.

Jarrod's heart went out to Isabelle. No wonder she appeared to be shrinking into herself under the verbal assault.

"Warned her about what exactly?" Jarrod asked. Did Heather know something she wasn't telling?

"Heirs coming out of the woodwork," Heather retorted. "You see it all the time when someone rich passes away. All of a sudden, there are more relatives around than ever came to a family reunion. Isabelle and I are Davis's only heirs. That was his intention, and that's the way it should be."

"Do you think . . ." Thomas swallowed hard and stared at Heather. "I didn't even know I was adopted until Isabelle showed up. I'm certainly not after anyone's money."

"So you say now." Heather gripped the arms of the chair as if to keep herself from flying across the table and attacking Thomas. "But I'll bet you change your tune when you see what you're missing out on."

Thomas shifted to Isabelle. "You don't believe that, do you?"

"Of course not," Isabelle said firmly. "Though what I do with my inheritance is no one's business but my own. And if I choose to share some of it with my long-lost brother, then I will."

"I don't want your money," Thomas insisted. "We're doing fine." He paused and took a deep breath. "All I want is the truth."

Jarrod jumped in to take control of the conversation before Heather went on another rant. "Then you agree to take the DNA test?"

"Absolutely," Thomas said. "I want to know if Isabelle and I are related." He faced Heather, and his expression hardened. "And not because of any inheritance."

Heather grunted but didn't say anything. Instead, she examined her manicure as if to indicate she was done with the conversation.

K. C. waved her hand. "Can I say something?"

"Be my guest," Jarrod replied.

"I totally agree that Thomas and Isabelle need to find out if they're related. It would also be great to solve the mystery of this Michelle Blacke, whoever she may be." K. C. showered all of them with a politician's perfect conciliatory smile. "But could we please take a moment to consider the consequences of this revelation?"

"What do you mean?" Jarrod asked.

"This will sound selfish, I know." K. C. rested a hand on her husband's arm. "I'm sorry to even bring it up. Truly I am. But we can't forget that I'm running in a very competitive race. Whether or not Thomas is a

Byrnes, if the opposition finds out he's taking a DNA test, there is no telling what kind of spin they would put on that information, and that could harm my campaign."

"I don't think you have anything to worry about," Thomas said soothingly as he clasped K. C.'s hand. "There's nothing scandalous about finding out you're adopted and searching for your family."

"Which is why you're not my campaign manager," K. C. teased, then cast a pleading glance at Jarrod. "Surely you can understand. Given your line of work, you must see how facts are often twisted to frame a false narrative and how difficult it can be to correct that narrative once it's released to the public."

"I suppose," Jarrod assented. "But I also agree with Thomas. This could be a good thing for your campaign if you get ahead of it."

"I'm sure you mean well," K. C. said. "But we've worked too long and hard to make any rookie mistakes now. You'd be amazed at how my opponent has taken the most benign social media posts and used them as ammunition against me."

"What are you saying?" Jarrod asked.

K. C. pressed her lips together and focused on Isabelle. "All I'm asking is that you wait until after the election to take the test. And not to let anyone know that you even plan to take such a test." She smiled at Thomas and covered their clasped hands with her free one. "That's not too much to ask for, is it? When we've already come so far."

"It means that much to you for me to wait?" Thomas asked.

"We already have so many things on our plate," K. C. said. "The election is a few weeks away. After that, you and Isabelle can take the test, and if you're related after all, we can plan a formal announcement. We'll have PR people who can make the most of it."

"You're not turning my DNA test into a circus sideshow," Thomas said, his expression flickering from support to disgust.

"I didn't mean it like that," K. C. soothed. "The PR team will know what to say in a press release. You've gone all your life not knowing about your biological family. Can't you wait a little longer? Please."

"I suppose," Thomas said. "What do you think, Isabelle?"

"If that's what you want, of course." She gave him a warm smile. "I'm not here to stir up trouble."

"Heather?" K. C. asked. "Would you be willing to keep this a secret?"

"I won't be telling anyone." Heather practically spat the words. "This is all a big mistake. You'll see."

"Mum's the word then." K. C. ignored Heather's grumbling and smiled at the others. "Is there anything else we need to discuss today? If not, I need to go. No matter the weather or the circumstances, campaigns don't run by themselves."

Jarrod didn't comment on the group's decision, but K. C., apparently pleased with herself for getting her way, didn't seem to notice. That was okay. If she thought she had his promise, then she was mistaken. He wouldn't go out of his way to let anyone know about the possible relationship between Thomas Reid and wealthy philanthropist Davis Byrnes or about the DNA tests that Thomas and Isabelle would be taking. But if this family secret had anything to do with Jasper's shooting, then Jarrod refused to be held to a promise he couldn't keep. Finding out who had shot Jasper was his number one priority—not locating Isabelle's lost sibling. And certainly not the ins and outs of a political campaign.

Jarrod had to admit that Heather made a good point. Isabelle appeared to be desperate to locate a relative. Maybe it was because she was grieving her father or she was simply lonely. But having the same birth date as Baby Girl Blacke was only circumstantial evidence at this point. No compelling evidence existed that Isabelle wasn't who she had always believed herself to be before she discovered the mysterious birth certificates—the biological daughter of Davis Byrnes and his beloved late wife.

The best he could do for Isabelle was to prove her parentage, one way or the other. And perhaps the best way to do that was to find out more about Michelle Blacke.

Or, perhaps more precisely, Morgan Young.

The results of Jarrod's deep dive weren't a surprise. He'd started with the conclusion that Michelle Blacke and Morgan Young were one and the same, and it hadn't taken him long to prove exactly that.

It wasn't his preferred investigative approach. In fact, he considered any kind of bias to be dangerous to a proper investigation. It was much better to discard any preconceived conclusions and let the puzzle pieces form their own picture. But in this case, when time was of the essence, he made an exception to his own rule.

Not surprisingly, Michelle Blacke had disappeared about the same time an adult Morgan Young sprang into being. The two women had different social security numbers, but that didn't prove they were two different individuals. Morgan Young may have managed to obtain a false identity. What was still disconcerting, though, was that Michelle Blacke had also sprung into being as an adult.

Jarrod could find no record of either woman as a child.

Alone in his office, he discovered driver's license photos for both Morgan and Michelle, and he uploaded them to a facial recognition program. Not surprisingly, the photos were of the same woman.

Jarrod picked up a printout of Morgan's photo. "Now I know

the truth," he said to the picture. "Isabelle was right. You are Michelle Blacke. But who were you before you took that name?"

The woman in the photo simply stared back at him, a Mona Lisa smile on her face.

Jarrod entered Morgan's address into his GPS app and drove to the north shore of the island. He parked in a lot across the street from her house and waited, hoping to catch her coming or going.

He glanced at the boardwalk that led across the sand dunes to the beach. The wind had picked up, and the dark skies threatened more rain. The brewing storm out in the Atlantic had stalled for the moment, and the meteorologists were mixed in their forecasts of what path it would take when it started moving again.

The doomsday experts warned of the imminent need for evacuation. But most of the islanders had survived low category storms before. Unless this one grew into a category 4 or 5, it was doubtful more than a handful of people would retreat to the mainland.

It wasn't that the islanders were fools or careless of their lives. In the past, they'd experienced enough damage to understand how dangerous a hurricane could be. But they weren't in a hurry to leave their homes either, at least not until the storm neared destructive speeds.

The odd mindset was little understood by those who didn't live in coastal areas and one Jarrod no longer tried to explain to friends and colleagues from the central states.

He saw Morgan pull into her driveway. She drove a black Pontiac Vibe that had to be at least ten years old since Pontiacs weren't even made anymore. She turned off the car but remained in the driver's seat, gazing out the windshield.

Jarrod jumped out of his SUV, hurried across the street, and tapped on her car's passenger window.

Startled, Morgan jerked her head toward the sound, then frowned. She unlocked the car doors.

He slid into the passenger seat.

"Are you following me?" she asked.

"I'm curious about you," Jarrod replied.

"I'm sure you know all about the dangers of curiosity."

"'Curiosity killed the cat, but satisfaction brought it back.'"

Morgan stared at him. "Well said. Though I wonder if your brother's clients are always satisfied with the results of his detective work. Or if they sometimes wish they had drowned their curiosity before they peeked under stones best left alone."

"Maybe. But right now, I'm only interested in the curiosity of one of Jasper's clients. Especially if that's why he ended up in the hospital."

"You think I had something to do with that?"

"I don't know." Jarrod opened his phone to the photos of the birth certificates. "What do you know about these?" He handed his phone to Morgan.

She focused on the screen, zooming in on different aspects of the two certificates. "Where did you get these?"

"I think you know that."

"The young woman who was at Jasper's office yesterday," Morgan responded. "She said her name was Isabelle Byrnes."

"And your name is Michelle Blacke," Jarrod said evenly, careful not to sound accusatory. He hoped Morgan—Michelle—would see he meant her no harm. "Or at least, it used to be."

Her shoulders slumped, and she turned her head, avoiding Jarrod's eyes.

"I guess the next question is," he continued, "who is Baby Girl Blacke?"

Morgan faced him, and her lips curved into a sad smile. "Don't pretend you don't already know."

"Isabelle."

"She's a lovely young woman." Her voice changed to a slightly teasing tone. "Wouldn't you agree?"

Jarrod realized there was no use denying it. "She is. She favors you."

"I'm immune to flattery."

"It's not flattery if it's true." He took his phone from her. "And Baby Boy Blacke? Is that Thomas Reid?"

"How much does Isabelle know?"

"She and Thomas have talked about the possibility that they're siblings. They want to take DNA tests to be sure. But in deference to Mrs. Reid's request, that won't happen until after the election."

"I suppose the tests are a good idea, but they're not necessary." Morgan played with a ring on her right hand, twisting it around her finger. The corded band was set with a diamond solitaire surrounded by two deep-blue stones. "Jasper said K. C. appeared to be overwhelmed by the news. Apparently, she didn't appreciate finding out her husband had been adopted. Or that his real parents were unmarried college dropouts."

Jarrod blinked. He was usually skilled at hiding his reactions, but he hadn't been prepared for this revelation. He wanted to know more about Morgan's story, but that could wait. "Are you saying K. C. knew about the adoption before today?"

"That's what Jasper told me." She smiled faintly. "You could say we're business associates, Jasper and me. Sometimes I do legal work for him. He'd told K. C. about the adoption before he learned of my connection. Once he did, he called me."

"Is that why you were at his office yesterday?"

"I'd been out of town for a few days. I returned yesterday and went straight to his office." Sadness filled her voice. "I didn't know about the shooting. I'm so sorry."

Jarrod appreciated her sympathy, but his primary focus needed to be on the information she'd given him. It didn't make sense. "If K. C. already knew about the adoption, why did she act so surprised when Isabelle and I talked to her and Thomas this morning?"

"I couldn't say." Morgan met his gaze, her expression thoughtful. "My guess is that she hadn't told Thomas. Maybe she didn't want him to know she already knew."

She had a point, but Jarrod couldn't help thinking K. C.'s reasons went deeper than an attempt to deceive her husband. It was true that she was an ambitious politician, but why would that cause her to try to hide her husband's true parentage?

And how far would she go to keep it a secret?

Isabelle parked Heather's Audi half a block away from the clinic where Thomas had asked her to meet him. She'd been honest with her stepmother about why she needed to borrow the car. Heather had resisted at first—no surprise there—but she relented when Isabelle got on her phone to schedule a ride. She was still grumbling as Isabelle left the suite.

While Isabelle waited, she glanced around for Jarrod or Dax. She suspected one of them might have followed her, though she'd tried to be on the lookout for a tail on the drive over. But she didn't see either of them anywhere.

At least the rain had stopped again. The latest weather report indicated the storm had once more stalled offshore. Hopefully, it would stay away from the coast until it wore itself out and died.

Thomas's earlier phone call had both surprised and pleased her. Despite K. C.'s objections, he didn't want to wait until after the election to know the truth about their relationship. The clinic's physician was Thomas's boyhood friend who'd agreed to conduct the tests after the rest of the staff had left for the day

A sleek Mercedes pulled in front of the Audi, and Thomas emerged from the driver's side. He waved at Isabelle and waited for her to join him on the sidewalk.

"Thanks for agreeing to this on such short notice," he said. "No matter what K. C. thinks, I can't believe that in this day and age, voters care whether or not I was adopted."

"She does appear to be pretty sensitive about it," Isabelle said, maneuvering around puddles in the sidewalk as they walked toward the clinic.

"This race is very important to her," Thomas said. "To us."

Isabelle wasn't sure of his sincerity from the way he added those last two words. It sounded as if he'd said them because they were expected rather than because he really meant them. But that was conjecture on her part. She couldn't presume to know the true feelings of a man she'd only recently met.

Except he was so much like her father, and at times she felt as if she'd known him for years.

"Anyway, you should probably know that I didn't tell K. C. I'm doing this." He stopped on the sidewalk.

She stopped beside him, unsure how to respond.

"If you talk to her, I'd appreciate it if you didn't mention it," Thomas continued. "I'll tell her when we get the results."

"I won't say anything," Isabelle promised. A strange thrill went up her spine as if the two of them were naughty children keeping a secret from the grown-ups. A connection threaded them together in this moment, a connection that may have been stolen from them by circumstances neither of them knew anything about.

She also felt a little guilty. It was possible she was Thomas's sister, but K. C. was his wife. Isabelle shouldn't encourage him to keep secrets from her. In any other circumstance, she wouldn't.

But Isabelle was as anxious as Thomas to discover the truth. It seemed particularly important when Jasper might have been shot because of her search. Knowing the truth about who they were could solve that mystery. The fewer people who knew what they were up to, the less likely it was to get back to the shooter.

Thomas led the way to the back of the clinic.

A man about his age stood at the rear door and stared at the sky.

"Finding shapes in those clouds to write about?" Thomas asked the other man.

"They're all one gray mass to the inexperienced. Yet notice the varying shades and the contours they reveal." The stranger flashed a smile at Isabelle. "Neil Macey, general practitioner and occasional poet."

"Isabelle Byrnes."

"Pleased to meet a friend of Thomas's." Neil opened the door and ushered them inside. "Though from what I understand, you may be more than a friend."

"That's what we're hoping to find out." Isabelle entered the examining room. "Thank you for doing this for us."

"Anything for Thomas," Neil said. "He sold me both my first and second houses, you know."

"That makes me sound much more impressive than I am," Thomas confessed to Isabelle.

"No, it's an accurate representation. You're much more impressive than you let on." Neil's good-natured chuckle helped to put them both at ease in this bizarre situation. "He's a real estate agent, and that's what they do. But both times he managed to find the house I didn't know I wanted until he showed it to me. It's like he knows me better than I know myself."

"Well, we spent practically all our free time together as kids," Thomas said. "That is, until we started spending time with girls."

Neil laughed again. "Those were the good old days. Thomas and I were neighbors growing up. We took turns eating supper at each other's houses, especially in the summer. We were like brothers." He raised an eyebrow at Isabelle, and his eyes twinkled with fun as he added, "And now here you are, threatening to break up our dynamic duo."

"Not at all," Isabelle said. "I'm an only child too, and I wouldn't mind finding out I had a sibling."

Neil grew serious. "You couldn't ask for a better one than this guy right here." He patted Thomas's shoulder. "When you first told me you were adopted, I thought you must be crazy. I never would have guessed."

"Sometimes I wondered," Thomas admitted. "But it's still . . . I don't know how to explain it."

"What do your parents think of all this?" Neil asked.

"They're being supportive," Thomas replied. "And they shared the little information they have. But I haven't told them or anyone else about taking this DNA test."

"Not even K. C.?" Neil asked.

"Especially not K. C." Thomas shrugged. "She's got enough on her mind with the campaign. You know how preoccupied she gets. We'll deal with the results once we know what they are. There's no reason to get everyone all worked up when we don't know anything for sure."

"Probably the best plan." Neil picked up one of the two DNA testing packets on the counter. "Who wants to go first?"

Isabelle and Thomas exchanged glances, then laughed.

Just standing beside her potential brother made her giddy. But it also made her heart ache with grief that Dad couldn't meet Thomas or answer their questions. He wasn't around to explain why Thomas had been given to strangers. Why Isabelle had stayed with him.

"I will," Thomas volunteered. "I'm older."

"What difference does that make?" Isabelle asked, feigning petulance.

"I can show you how it's done," Thomas teased. "In case you're squeamish."

"Which I'm not. Except when it comes to brown lizards. I don't mind the green ones. But the brown ones?" She shivered. "Yuck."

"I know exactly what you mean," Thomas said. "The green ones are friendly, but the brown ones always act like they're up to something."

Another shared connection, albeit an odd one. But wasn't that what it was like to be a family? To share one another's quirks and phobias?

The circumstances behind their births and adoptions didn't matter. With all her heart, Isabelle wanted the DNA tests to prove they were related.

Then she would have a brother. And she wouldn't be alone.

Once the tests were administered, Isabelle lingered at the office while Thomas and Neil regaled her with stories from their boyhood days on the island. Both were avid fishermen and surfers. At least they were until family and professional obligations had overtaken their lives.

Isabelle found it comforting to see Thomas interacting with someone who'd known him all his life. Their conversation gave her another glimpse into his character. His ease with his friend showed him to be a man comfortable in his own skin, content with his life, and proud of his family.

She was relieved to know that Thomas was a good guy. It was so much better than finding out she was related to an awful person. A few of her clients had been appalled to discover the rotten apples in their family trees. Isabelle had always been sympathetic, but this experience with Thomas increased her understanding of how those clients must have felt.

That old saying that curiosity killed the cat seemed to apply at times. Most people didn't know how the saying ended—that satisfaction brought it back. Isabelle hoped that it proved true and she wouldn't end up regretting her search for answers.

After saying goodbye to Neil, Thomas and Isabelle returned to their vehicles. The rain still held off, and the sun shone weakly through the gray mass of clouds. It was impossible to see the ocean from where they were because of the trees and buildings that stood between them and the horizon. But Isabelle could imagine the dark waves pounding onto the beach.

Thomas hesitated, then hugged Isabelle. For a second, she could almost believe she was in her father's arms again.

The moment was interrupted by a shout from across the street.

Thomas immediately straightened and stepped away from her, muttering, "Oh, great."

"Who is it?" she asked.

A spindly twentysomething man with a mop of red curls jaywalked across the street toward them. "Thomas, wait up."

"I'm not going anywhere," Thomas said in a singsong voice. When the man approached them, Thomas introduced him to Isabelle. "This is Robert Larson, K. C.'s campaign manager."

"Pleased to meet you," Isabelle said.

"Same here," the man said, eyeing Isabelle, then Thomas, and finally the clinic with suspicion. "What brings you out in this weather? It must have been something important."

"Isabelle is from out of town," Thomas said with a wave at the nearby shops and offices. "I've been showing her around."

"Is that so?" Robert asked. "Maybe you should have done your hugging before you walked out on the street."

"You're not trying to insinuate anything, are you?" Thomas asked.

Isabelle was shocked. "You don't think we're—"

"Not me," Robert interrupted. "I know Thomas better than that.

But these other people around here?" He gestured at the empty street as if it were crowded with onlookers. "They love to gossip. And the opposition doesn't need more than a spark of scandal to fan into a flame. None of us wants that."

"You worry too much," Thomas said, obviously annoyed and ill at ease. "K. C. knows I'm with Isabelle. It's no big deal."

Isabelle wanted to say something to help, but her mind was a blank. Besides, protesting too much might be worse than not protesting at all.

"Whatever you say." Robert let his gaze linger on the clinic. "No big deal at all."

A gust of wind blew past them, and huge splatters of rain pounded the sidewalk.

"Come on," Thomas said as he gripped Isabelle's arm. "The storm's coming back."

As he pulled her away from Robert, she glanced over her shoulder. The man stood on the sidewalk as if oblivious to the driving rain and watched them.

"He knows," Isabelle said.

"It's okay," Thomas answered. "I should have told K. C. instead of trying to hide it. The important thing is that I tell her before he does."

"Any regrets?" Isabelle asked.

"None." Thomas smiled at her.

His smile was so much like her father's that it took all her willpower not to embrace him in a tight, familial hug. "Me either," she whispered.

In the comfort of Thomas's brotherly presence, Isabelle pushed away all thoughts of cruel notes, black petals, and severed brakes.

But only for a moment. The threat was still out there, as deadly as the storm brewing offshore.

Isabelle didn't like sneaking out of the hotel, but what other choice did she have? K. C. had insisted they meet alone. After the fit Heather had thrown last night, Isabelle knew her stepmother would never let that happen.

When Isabelle had returned from the clinic, Heather had made it clear that she didn't trust Thomas or K. C. to accept that Davis hadn't mentioned any unknown relatives in his will. Heather was certain that if Isabelle explored the possibility of sharing even a small amount of her wealth with the Reids, the estate would be tied up in litigation for months or years. The cost of that litigation might decrease the value of the estate, thus decreasing the sum total of Heather's share.

Isabelle's response that she might offer a percentage of her share of the estate to Thomas if the DNA results proved he was her brother merely fueled on Heather's wrath. Isabelle thought Heather's ire was unwarranted. After all, that kind of arrangement wouldn't affect Heather's inheritance.

They'd ended up ordering room service, eating in silence while watching home renovation shows on TV, then retreating to their individual rooms.

Isabelle switched her television on to the same channel and crawled into bed. She'd had a long, emotional day beginning with the news of her tampered brakes. That had been followed by meeting Thomas and K. C., Thomas's parents, and finally making the trip with Thomas to the clinic.

Isabelle's physical aches added to her emotional turmoil. Her chest, arms, and muscles were still sore from the accident. As she propped up the pillows behind her, she checked her phone for a message from Jarrod. Nothing. They'd talked earlier on her drive from the clinic, a call that had thrilled her as if they were teenagers. It had been hard to say goodbye when she got to the bridge, but she needed all her focus to harness her fear and cross the expanse. Later, she realized she hadn't mentioned the confrontation with Robert Larson. But what did that matter?

While the television droned, Isabelle had reflected on Heather's unreasonable anger. Perhaps her anger came from a lack of security she'd experienced as a child. Heather rarely spoke of her past, but Isabelle had picked up a detail here and there through the years. Heather's father had abandoned his family, and her mother moved them from one town to another in a search for . . . what? Isabelle didn't have a clue, though she pitied anyone who didn't have strong family roots to provide structure and identity.

These days, Isabelle felt that she had the right to wallow in that pity herself. Her family tree wasn't as solid and secure as she'd always believed. All those past generations of Byrneses might have nothing to do with her. Yet they'd influenced everything she'd always known about herself. They'd even influenced her choice of career.

What if it turned out she wasn't a Byrnes after all? How would she find her authentic identity?

Now these same gloomy thoughts surrounded her when she slipped out of the suite—thankful that Heather was still in her bedroom—to meet K. C. in the hotel café. Despite her own unsettled emotions, Isabelle hoped this meeting would give her the opportunity to soothe K. C.'s ruffled feathers. Maybe she'd have better luck reconciling with Thomas's wife than with her own stepmother.

When Isabelle reached the ground floor, she started across the lobby toward the café, then noticed K. C. rising from a nearby chair. Despite the inclement weather, K. C. was impeccably dressed in a tailored pantsuit. Her makeup was fresh, and not a hair was out of place.

Even as she wondered how K. C. had managed such a feat, Isabelle veered toward her with a smile. "Do you think this rain will ever stop?" she asked with a light chuckle. "I heard on the news this morning that the storm is on the move again."

"I heard that too," K. C. responded. She seemed to appraise Isabelle from head to toe and back again. And to find her wanting.

Isabelle glanced down at her outfit, a classic tunic over leggings and ankle boots she'd thrown on after receiving K. C.'s call. She self-consciously patted the messy bun she'd pulled her hair into before tiptoeing from the suite.

"Shall we go to the café?" Isabelle asked. "I've fallen in love with their chocolate croissants, even though it means more time on the treadmill."

"I have another idea." K. C.'s steady gaze bored into Isabelle's soul. "Let's go for a ride."

A chill raced up Isabelle's spine, but she did her best to suppress it. "I didn't bring a jacket." Or a bag or even her phone.

"You won't need one." K. C. strode along a corridor, leaving Isabelle no choice but to follow her. "I'm parked in the garage."

"I thought the garage was for guests." Isabelle recalled her room key doubled as a pass to raise the barrier at the entrance ramp when she'd returned to the garage with Heather's car.

"Is that so?" K. C. smirked. "Power is an incredible tonic. Sometimes I wonder if it's not more potent than money. Perhaps you would disagree. I doubt you've ever known what it's like to be without either."

Isabelle let K. C.'s words roll around in her thoughts, dissecting and digesting them at the same time. The woman obviously disliked her. But why? Perhaps Thomas had told her about their taking the DNA tests. Would she blame Isabelle for that? Maybe. It was probably easier for her to lash out at a stranger than her husband.

But that conversation—any conversation—could take place in the hotel café or lobby. Where was K. C. taking her?

K. C. pushed open the heavy metal door leading to the cavernous parking garage.

Isabelle followed her down the stairs, then stopped. "If you have something to say to me, say it here." Not surprisingly, her voice had a slight tremor. She didn't want to start off on the wrong foot with the person who might be her sister-in-law. But what if . . . "Did you leave me those notes?"

"What do you mean?" K. C. asked as she stared at her. "What notes?"

"I think you know." Isabelle crossed her arms, determined not to take another step until she got answers. "I heard you're in a gardening club. Do you happen to have a fondness for black tulips?"

"I have no idea what you're talking about."

"Of course you don't." Isabelle's voice grew stronger, as did her certitude that she was right. "But as you can see, I don't scare that easily. I came here to find answers, and I think I have." She blinked back sudden tears. This wasn't a conversation she'd expected to have. That she even wanted to have. "Would it really be all that bad to find out Thomas and I are related? That you and I might be family?"

"Thomas already has a family," K. C. said, her tone frigid. "He doesn't need you coming here and upsetting everything we've built together."

More chills raced up Isabelle's spine. "I don't want to upset anything—"

"Now you're making these baseless accusations about notes and tulips," K. C. interrupted. "There's no such thing as a black tulip."

Isabelle wrapped her arms around herself and shivered. The garage walls kept out the wind, but the air was still chilly. She was cold and not just from K. C.'s icy demeanor. Apparently, she was also too upset to think clearly. K. C. couldn't have sent the notes. The woman didn't even know of Isabelle's existence until yesterday. Only someone who knew Isabelle had rented the cottage and when she planned to arrive could have left the note and the black flowers.

"I'm sorry," Isabelle said. "I shouldn't have accused you of something you couldn't have done."

"At least we got that out of the way," K. C. replied. "Now let's go."

"Go where?"

"A special place." K. C. smiled toward the wall behind Isabelle. Her tone grew more chipper as she stepped closer and tapped Isabelle's arm. "It was meant to be a surprise, but Thomas will be there. Please come."

Isabelle hugged herself tighter. She liked most people, but she did not like K. C. Something about Thomas's wife was off. Yet she was a public servant with lofty goals and a well-known person in her community. Surely, K. C. was someone to trust and respect. Isabelle had been wrong to falsely accuse her. Maybe she was wrong to dislike her too. On the other hand, a warning alarm went off frantically deep inside her. But why?

K. C. tugged Isabelle by the arm. "Come on, or we'll be late. I'm parked right over there." She raised her key fob, and the lights flashed on a nearby luxury sedan.

Perhaps it was because of K. C.'s unyielding hold on Isabelle's arm. Or maybe the false note of her sudden eagerness sounded an alarm. Whatever the cause, Isabelle's instinct caused her to try to pull away.

K. C. wouldn't release her arm. "Come with me now."

"Let go of me," Isabelle demanded.

K. C. glanced behind Isabelle again, and a self-satisfied smile tugged at her lips.

Isabelle turned to look over her shoulder. A shadow appeared behind her. Suddenly her face was covered with a damp cloth. She fought to get away, to breathe.

But her senses dulled until she slipped into darkness.

When Isabelle woke, she found herself sitting in an upholstered chair with her hands tied in front of her. The heavy drapes covering the front picture window allowed little light into the room. Rain pelted against the glass, and the wind howled outside. Isabelle tried to stand, but she immediately stumbled back into the chair. Her feet were also bound.

She blinked and tried to calm down.

Her eyes had barely adjusted to the dark when K. C. entered and flipped a switch, illuminating a nearby lamp. "Good. You're awake."

Given her circumstances, Isabelle surprisingly didn't feel afraid but irritated. She glared at K. C. "What do you think you're doing?"

"Keeping you away from my husband."

Isabelle let that sink in. K. C. hadn't been working alone, but her words indicated that Thomas hadn't been her accomplice. Relief flooded through her at that realization. She'd have been heartbroken if Thomas had been a part of this. Even though they didn't know the results of the DNA tests yet, she felt a connection with him that went beyond a mere hope that he was her brother. She only prayed that connection wasn't a false hope based on how much she missed her dad—and how much Thomas reminded her of him.

If Thomas wasn't part of this abduction or whatever K. C. was doing, then who was? The campaign manager. Robert Larson. He'd given Isabelle an uneasy feeling when he'd confronted her and Thomas outside the clinic yesterday.

She was alone in the room with K. C. Maybe Robert was elsewhere in the house. Waiting. Listening.

Her earlier irritation gave into a sliver of fear. K. C. didn't seem dangerous. She certainly wouldn't want to do anything to sully her reputation or get her hands dirty. But what about Robert?

Isabelle wouldn't be here, hands and feet tied together, if Robert didn't wish her harm. And why? Just because she might be Thomas's sister? How could that possibly matter?

Jarrod punched the number on the elevator's panel for Isabelle's floor. He rubbed his jaw, scratching his fingers against the stubble there. Maybe he should have taken the time to shower and shave before dropping by unannounced.

But Jarrod had been jolted from sleep by Olivia's frantic phone call in the wee hours of the morning. After an uneventful day when his brother's monitors indicated steady improvement, leading the family to cautiously hope for a positive prognosis, Jasper had unexpectedly gone into cardiac arrest.

Jarrod had spent the last several hours alternately pacing the corridors of the intensive care unit and trying to reassure Olivia that everything was going to be fine—a reassurance they pretended to believe for each other's sake despite the fear that engulfed them.

Thankfully, the medical team's heroic efforts, bolstered by Jarrod's and Olivia's prayers, eventually stabilized Jasper's condition. Once the crisis had passed, Jarrod persuaded Olivia to go home. He'd stayed with Jasper, dozing in the chair, until Olivia's father arrived and sent him away.

The elevator doors opened, and Jarrod made his way to Isabelle's suite. She had called him the previous evening while driving back to the hotel after her clandestine trip to the clinic. Her spirits were positively buoyant as she shared how Thomas had teased that he should take the test first because he was the older of the two. They were obviously drawn to each other, as if they somehow already knew in their hearts that they shared the same genes, that they were family.

She'd sounded so hopeful about the results that Jarrod had experienced a strange stirring in his gut. It couldn't be jealousy—he wasn't interested in being Isabelle's brother.

The sick feeling eased, crowded out by warmth and longing. Their phone call hadn't lasted long, definitely not as long as Jarrod would have liked. Not surprisingly, Isabelle didn't want to be on the phone while driving across the bridge. Jarrod had let her go and resisted the urge to call her again. But it hadn't been easy. He didn't even get the chance to tell her that he had proof Michelle Blacke and Morgan Young were the same person.

At least he knew she'd arrived safely at the hotel. Samantha, his security agent who'd gotten Heather's photograph a couple of days before, had tailed Isabelle from the hotel to the clinic and back again. He'd swatted away the pang of guilt for his subterfuge. Isabelle wouldn't like being followed.

Maybe it was that guilt that compelled Jarrod to drive from the hospital to the hotel instead of going home. The reason why he hadn't called Isabelle first to see if she minded an unexpected visit. He shook his head. Guilt was an excuse. The truth was, he ached to see her. To *be* with her. Especially after the roller coaster he'd been on for the past several hours.

If Jasper's condition hadn't stabilized, Jarrod would have given all his strength to support his sister-in-law in her grief. But who would have been there for him? For practically the first time in Jarrod's life, the acute pain of being alone during a family crisis squeezed his heart. He had no delusions that Isabelle desired that heavy role. Yet in the aftermath of Jasper's crisis, Jarrod felt inexplicably drawn to her. Even if he didn't tell her about the frightening hours when his thoughts were consumed by his brother's welfare, her mere presence would boost his spirits.

As he stood outside the door to her suite, he rubbed his jaw again. It wasn't too late to return to his SUV and go home. Get a few hours of needed sleep. Start fresh on his search for Jasper's shooter.

In spite of his haggard appearance, the desire to stay won out over his instinct to leave, the insistent reminder that Isabelle was his brother's client and, by default, someone who should be off-limits to even the hint of attraction.

If only his heart would listen.

Jarrod rapped on the door, barely aware that he held his breath while waiting for it to open. When he heard the click of the dead bolt and the sliding of the chain, he made a conscious effort to relax his shoulders. It was too late to think of anything witty to say as an explanation for why he was there, so he hoped a smile would be enough.

The door opened, and he stifled a sigh. Of course, Heather would be the one to answer the door.

Heather stared at him, her eyes guarded. She wore an oversize sweater and yoga pants with fluffy slippers. "Isabelle didn't tell me that you were coming by," she said, surprise brightening her tone.

"She didn't know." Jarrod peered over Heather's head, hoping to see Isabelle. "Mind if I come in?"

"Sure." She opened the door wider and gestured for him to enter. "We should have a talk."

Put on alert by her words, he stayed in the corridor. What could he and Heather possibly have to talk about? "We?"

"You're a smart guy. Surely you can see Izzy is still grieving the death of her father." Heather swiped at an invisible tear. "We both are. Davis was a remarkable man. It's too bad you didn't have a chance to meet him. The two of you would have gotten along so well."

Jarrod wasn't sure how to respond to her gushing words. Davis Byrnes was a well-known philanthropist in the region but not necessarily a household name. If Jarrod wasn't in the security field, he probably wouldn't have known of his existence until Isabelle's dramatic entrance into his life. He put as much sympathy in his voice as he could while remaining on guard. "I'm sorry I didn't get that chance."

Her hands fluttered to her mouth. "Where are my manners? Would you like a cup of coffee or tea?"

"No thank you, but would you let Isabelle know I'm here?"

Heather feigned a laugh. "Didn't I tell you? She's gone."

A cold twinge of fear zipped along his spine. "Where is she?"

"Izzy has been so secretive lately." She gave an exaggerated shrug. "How would I know?"

"When did she leave?" Jarrod demanded. "Did she take your car?"

"I'm not her keeper." Heather headed for the suite's seating area. "But you're welcome to wait for her to return."

Jarrod grabbed his phone and called Isabelle's number. After a few rings, it went to voice mail. He tried again with the same result.

He frantically typed a text. *Call me.*

His next call was to Samantha. Again, no response.

Jarrod strode into the suite.

Heather was sitting on the sofa, twirling a key ring on her index finger. "I guess she walked to wherever she went."

"You don't seem concerned." He could barely contain his frustration, which now bordered on anger. Isabelle had disappeared, and her stepmother was providing no help.

"I warned her about those stupid birth certificates." She may have intended a playful tone, but a sharp edge grated her words. "Davis obviously kept them a secret for a reason. If he had wanted Izzy to know about them, he would have given them to her long ago. Or at least mentioned them."

His thoughts tumbled with possibilities and impossibilities. Was

Morgan Young aka Michelle Blacke involved in Jasper's shooting, the black petals, and the sabotaged brakes? Or was K. C.—perhaps the entire Reid family—complicit in some strange scheme to prevent Isabelle from learning the truth about her family?

Heather dropped the key ring onto the coffee table. "That family is ridiculously crazy about knowing everything there is to know about their ancestors, like who married who and the names of the children and where they're all buried." She gave a harsh laugh. "Even I can usually guess at that. Most of them are buried in a private cemetery. They still have their own private cemetery with all these Byrnes and offshoots of Byrnes buried on the estate."

"Where's Isabelle?" Jarrod asked again. It took all of his self-control to keep his voice level.

"I don't know, and I don't care." She stretched her legs out along the couch. "Davis, though? He's buried right next to Izzy's mother. Forever and eternity. That tells you all you need to know about how much he cared for me."

Jarrod rubbed the back of his neck while his mind raced. Heather's ramblings weren't helping him focus, and that was exactly what he needed to do. Right now, all that mattered was finding Isabelle.

Without another word to Heather, he left the suite and paced the corridor, willing himself to concentrate.

Maybe Isabelle was still in the hotel. Perhaps she was sitting in the café where they had talked to Thomas and K. C., and he hadn't noticed her when he came in. It was possible she was shopping in one of the hotel's boutique stores. Her phone could be on silent, so she could have missed his messages.

Or maybe she was in trouble.

He sent her another text, then called Thomas, skipping the formalities when Thomas picked up. "Is Isabelle with you?"

"No. Why?" Thomas clipped his words.

"Have you talked to her?"

"Not since yesterday."

It wasn't the answer Jarrod had hoped to hear.

"What's going on?" Thomas asked, a note of concern in his voice. "Is she okay? Did something happen?"

Jarrod forced himself to take a deep breath. He was a professional, and he needed to act like one instead of causing Thomas to needlessly worry when there was probably a simple explanation for Isabelle's absence.

"She's not in her hotel suite," he said, attempting to sound calm. "Her stepmother doesn't know where she is—"

"Some stepmother," Thomas huffed.

Jarrod agreed wholeheartedly, but professionalism prevented him from saying so. "She's probably here at the hotel somewhere." He wasn't sure whether he was trying to reassure Thomas or himself. "I'll do a search."

"What if you can't find her?"

Jarrod didn't want to face that possibility. Not until he had no other choice.

"What can I do?" Thomas asked. He sounded as helpless as Jarrod felt.

"Try not to worry." Jarrod had enough worry for both of them. "I'll call you as soon as I have news."

"I'm coming to the hotel," Thomas said firmly.

"There's no need for that."

"It's what a brother would do." His voice caught, and he cleared his throat loudly. "Isn't it?"

"You already have the results?" Jarrod hadn't intended to sound skeptical, but there was no way the tests could have been completed so quickly. Not that it mattered. Morgan had already admitted to being Thomas's and Isabelle's mother. But it wasn't Jarrod's place to share that news.

"I don't need a test to tell me what's true. I'm on my way." Thomas ended the call.

Jarrod hesitated outside the suite. Heather had already made it clear that she wasn't concerned about her stepdaughter. Nothing good could come from talking to her again. He continued to the elevator and pressed the button to call it.

As the door opened, his phone rang. His heart hitched, even though he didn't recognize the number. "Jarrod Long," he said.

"It's Morgan Young," a voice whispered.

The door started to close, and Jarrod held out his hand to stop it. "Is Isabelle with you?"

"I followed her." Morgan whispered an address, then made a strange sound, a cross between a surprised shriek and a muffled groan.

Sounds of a struggle came through the phone's microphone, then a hard slam as the call abruptly ended.

Jarrod stared at his phone screen as if it could show him what had happened to Morgan. He knew he needed to move, to act, to do something—anything. Yet it was as if his feet were rooted to the carpet.

The elevator door pushed against his hand, and he stumbled across the threshold. The action seemed to jump-start his brain. Morgan had followed Isabelle to the address she'd given him before the call ended. Jarrod jabbed the button for the lobby, then entered the address in the GPS tracker app on his phone. The address showed a sparsely populated area on the northern edge of the island.

Why would Isabelle have gone to that isolated spot, especially in this torrential rain? How would she even know such a secluded place existed?

When the elevator door opened, Jarrod sprinted toward the lobby, almost colliding with a bellman pushing a cartful of luggage. "Excuse me," Jarrod called over his shoulder as he took off again.

His phone sounded a text alert, and he paused to read Thomas's message. *Outside. Room number?*

Jarrod breathed a sigh of relief. He remembered from his background research on Thomas that the man had also served in the military. Jarrod would take all the help he could get.

He didn't take the time to reply to the text. Instead, he rushed outside, pulling his jacket collar around his neck as a strong gust of wind pushed against him. Headlights gleamed through the downpour. Recognizing Thomas's Mercedes, Jarrod waved at him, then ducked his head and ran toward the vehicle.

Thomas stopped the car.

Jarrod slid into the passenger seat and slammed the door against the rain. As he settled into the leather seat, he pushed his damp hair back from his forehead.

"What's going on?" Thomas put his car into gear. "Where to?"

Jarrod held out his phone so Thomas could see the screen. "I think Isabelle's here."

Thomas appeared skeptical. "What would she be doing there?"

"Drive," Jarrod ordered, then told him about Morgan's call. "It sounded like a scuffle, and the line went dead."

"Who's Morgan?" Thomas's face was grim, his focus on the rain-soaked streets as he maneuvered through the traffic and tried to avoid the deep puddles. "And why would they be at that house?"

Jarrod decided to ignore the first question. "No idea." He shrugged, heaved an irritated sigh, and tapped his phone. "I'll look up the owner." Why hadn't he done that while he was in the elevator?

"Don't bother," Thomas said. "I manage that property for a

couple of snowbirds who live in Indiana. They won't be here until after Thanksgiving."

Jarrod tried calling Isabelle and Morgan again, mostly to have something to do with his hands. A feeling of helplessness descended on him, as dark as the moment when he'd stepped into Jasper's office and found him lying on the floor, his life's blood pouring from his wound.

There had been nothing he could do to help his brother. What if there was nothing he could do to help Isabelle? Could he live with himself if he failed her as he'd failed Jasper?

Thunder rumbled, the boom echoing above the din of the downpour. Even if the houses at this end of the island were closer together, no one would be able to hear Isabelle's cries for help above the noise of the storm. Not that she intended to give K. C. the satisfaction of crying or begging to be set free. Somehow she'd find another way out of this nightmare.

Robert burst through the front door, dragging Morgan along with him. K. C. jumped from her seat as he propelled Morgan onto the couch. Blood trickled from her temple and matted her hair. One eye was practically swollen shut, and an ugly bruise was beginning to form.

A primal anger surged through Isabelle as she glared at Robert. "What did you do to her?"

"Shut up, or you'll get the same." He slammed the door behind him and shrugged off his yellow slicker. Water dripped onto the tile floor.

K. C. huffed, left the room, and returned with a towel.

To Isabelle's surprise, K. C. handed the towel to Robert instead of Morgan.

"Clean up your mess," K. C. told him.

"Morgan needs help." Isabelle struggled in vain to free her hands.

"I'm fine," Morgan said, her voice ragged. She gave Isabelle a weak smile. "Especially now that I know you're okay."

"Who are you?" K. C. demanded. "Robert, why did you bring her here?"

"Her name is Morgan Young. I found her outside." Robert dried his hair with the towel, then plopped down in a chair near the window. "She was on her cell."

"Is that name supposed to mean something to me?" K. C. was growing increasingly agitated. "Who was she talking to?"

"How would I know?" Robert snapped. "I smashed her phone."

K. C. turned to Morgan. "Apparently, you and Isabelle are friends. But you're going to regret getting involved in my personal affairs. Now tell me who you are and who you were talking to."

A self-satisfied smile slowly crossed Morgan's face. She used her jacket sleeve to stop the blood from her temple flowing onto her cheek.

Isabelle admired the woman's poise under such trying circumstances. Morgan showed no sign of fear. Isabelle resolved to demonstrate similar courage.

"I guess you could say I'm your mother-in-law," Morgan responded. "I realize I'm not what you expected. But you know what they say—you can choose your friends but not your family."

K. C. gasped.

"You're Thomas's mother?" Isabelle asked. Saying the words aloud confirmed what she already knew in her heart. "And mine?" She took a deep breath, preparing herself for Morgan's answer—whatever it might be.

"Yes, and yours." Morgan's smile deepened. She scooted to the end of the couch near Isabelle's chair and brushed her chilled fingers against Isabelle's cheek. "My sweet, lovely girl."

Isabelle was speechless.

"I never expected to know you or your brother except from a distance," Morgan said. "Davis and I had an agreement." A tear sparkled as it traveled down her cheek. "He made the arrangements for my babies."

"You're lying," K. C. blurted out. "Thomas's birth mother was Michelle Byrnes, and she died a long time ago."

Isabelle stilled her hands as she took in what K. C. was saying. "Wait a minute. Do you mean you already knew Thomas was adopted? Before yesterday?"

"Of course I knew," K. C. said, then gestured to Morgan. "How can you be Thomas's mother?"

Morgan winked at Isabelle with her good eye, then addressed K. C. "I changed my last name to Blacke when my father disowned me. You know, since I was the black sheep of the family and all. A year or so after Isabelle was born, I finally hit rock bottom. Thankfully, my big brother came to my rescue once again. Michelle Blacke 'died,' and Morgan Young was 'born.' He loved me more than I deserved."

"You mean my dad?" A surge of happiness buoyed Isabelle's spirits. She'd started out on her search filled with questions. Now they were being answered by the woman who'd given her life. "He was your brother."

"The best brother a gal could ever have," Morgan said.

"Oh, would you two stop it with all this hearts and flowers nonsense," K. C. snapped. She spun around to Robert. "You told me Thomas's mother died of a drug overdose. Yet here she is, as pretty as you please, very much alive."

"You can't blame me for that." Robert tossed the damp towel onto the floor. "I showed you a copy of the death certificate and the obituary. Someone went to a lot of trouble to make it look like she died."

"That was Davis and me." Morgan waved her hand. "I wanted a do-over. A new life. A new identity." She gazed at Isabelle with regret. "After all I'd put the family through, it seemed for the best."

Isabelle wanted to reach out to Morgan, take her hand, and tell her that she understood. But the ropes around her wrists made touch impossible, and the lump in her throat made it difficult to speak. She had trouble acknowledging the awful truth that Michelle Byrnes did not exist in their family tree. Her name, her date of birth, even her supposed date of death had been completely erased.

Isabelle found it hard to believe that her grandfather, a man who lived and breathed genealogy and insisted on detailed and accurate record keeping, was capable of such a deceit. Though maybe he wasn't the one who'd obliterated Michelle's existence. Maybe that had been done by Isabelle's father. But Isabelle found it equally difficult to put that onus on him. Dad was a principled lawyer and then a respected judge, sworn to uphold the law, to care about truth.

The painful insight seeped into her heart and took root. Dad had cared about truth, but he cared even more about Isabelle. He did everything in his power to convince her that she was loved and wanted, and he made sure she lacked for nothing. Almost all her childhood memories were happy ones.

He might have committed the necessary genealogical heresy to ensure Isabelle never found out that he was her uncle instead of her father. To do that, he'd cut his sister—someone else he loved and cherished—from the family tree.

Isabelle would probably never know why he'd held on to the birth certificates. Perhaps he simply couldn't bring himself to destroy the only remaining evidence of his sister's existence. Of the reality that she was the mom of two Byrnes babies. A son Davis watched from afar and a daughter he took into his own home.

"Lucky you." Sarcasm laced the words Robert directed toward Morgan. "You're going to get another chance to sacrifice yourself for your family."

K. C. crossed her arms over her chest. "Do you even have a plan? It's going to be difficult enough to fake Isabelle's suicide. Do you think anyone is going to believe that the two of them decided to kill themselves in the same place at the same time?"

Morgan gave Isabelle an encouraging smile. While K. C. and Robert were arguing, she mouthed, "It's going to be okay. I promise."

Isabelle gave a slight nod and prayed Morgan was right. She raised both hands to scratch her nose and realized the bonds didn't feel as tight as they had earlier. She rested her hands in her lap and studied the rope. As she slowly moved her fingers and wrists, the rope eased upward over her fingers.

"What are you going on about?" Robert asked K. C. "I thought we'd already agreed that your all-American good looks are going to get us into the governor's mansion someday, but I'm the brains and brawn behind that plan."

K. C. paced in front of the heavily draped picture window. "Your job was to find out everything you could about Thomas's biological family before I filed to run for this House seat. We were supposed to be prepared to handle any skeletons, remember? You assured me there weren't any to be found. You said his birth mother was dead, but she's obviously alive. His father was so forgettable he wasn't even named in any official documents. Is he going to show up here too?"

"Don't be ridiculous," Robert scoffed.

"But you promised me that no one else would find out my husband's parents were lowlife losers," K. C. reminded him. "I would have never married Thomas if I'd known he wasn't a true Reid. That family name and their connections mean something. How do you think I got on the county commission?"

Isabelle glanced at Morgan to see her reaction to K. C.'s comments, but her expression was impassive. Her head was tilted as if she were listening to something else and totally impervious to the insults being hurled at her.

Robert gave a harsh laugh. "You might as well tell them the entire plan. They're not going to live long enough to give it away."

"Let me guess," Morgan said. "You planned to tell Thomas about his connection to the Byrnes family sometime after K. C. won her election in the hope that he'd be reunited with his uncle and included as an heir."

"Thomas said he wasn't interested in my money," Isabelle protested.

"But K. C. and Robert are." Morgan propped her feet against the glass coffee table. "Very much so. Unfortunately, Davis died before K. C.'s dream scenario could come true."

"You're very perceptive." Robert stood and pulled a revolver from the back of his waistband. "That's why we've moved on to plan B. Thomas is an heir to Davis's fortune. With you and Isabelle out of the way, he'll inherit Isabelle's share. In a way, Davis did us all a favor by dying when he did."

If Isabelle's feet hadn't been bound, she would have jumped up and throttled Robert. She harnessed all her willpower to keep her hands locked together so he wouldn't know she was almost free of the rope.

Morgan, who must have sensed Isabelle's agitation, rested a comforting hand on her arm. "Exactly how do you plan to get rid of us?" Morgan asked Robert. Her voice was surprisingly calm. "It's not as easy to fake a suicide as you might believe. I read a lot of true crime stories—just for fun, you understand—and unintentional clues are always left behind."

"Not this time," Robert said, his tone filled with scorn. "You and Isabelle had a fight over money or because you abandoned her when she was a baby. The reason isn't all that important. You killed her, then, distraught over what you'd done, you killed yourself. Or maybe it was the other way around. It doesn't matter to me."

Isabelle fiddled again with the rope, freeing her hand and covering it with her other one so both appeared bound. Robert's casual talk of her and Morgan's deaths was unnerving. But Morgan's tranquil demeanor gave her needed strength. So did something inside herself—a peace that went beyond her understanding. She would not believe that God had brought Morgan and Thomas into her life, at a time when she needed them most, only to take her away from them.

Her thoughts drifted to Jarrod. He would never in a million years accept Robert's ridiculous murder-suicide story. And he'd never rest until he uncovered the truth. This certainty also gave her peace.

"Overconfidence will be your downfall," Morgan warned. "It often is for narcissists."

"You need to shut up," K. C. snapped at Morgan, then glared at Robert. "Stop waving that thing around. We need to do this now and get out of here."

Several streaks of lightning flashed outside the window, dazzling the room despite the drapes. They were followed closely by echoing claps of thunder that shook the small house.

Startled, Isabelle grabbed the arms of the chair, revealing she was no longer bound. But in the chaos, no one seemed to notice. Her senses were assaulted as everyone reacted to the light and noise.

K. C. squealed and rushed toward Robert as if seeking his protection. Morgan pushed the coffee table with her feet, hard enough that it fell on its side. The glass shattered, and K. C. shrieked. Robert held on to her with one arm while waving the gun around as if enemies waited in the shadows to assault him.

In one fluid motion, Morgan dropped to her knees beside Isabelle, grabbed a sliver of broken glass, and sawed at the ropes around Isabelle's ankles. Isabelle strained forward to help with the knots.

Robert's attention finally settled on them. Another lightning flash pierced the room. In the lingering brightness, his eyes glinted with rage.

"The lamp," Morgan said as the glass sliver severed the final rope.

Isabelle needed no further instruction. She grabbed the lamp beside the chair, yanking out the electrical cord from the wall. In the instant before the room went completely dark, she threw the lamp at Robert as he pointed the revolver at her. She hit the floor, covering Morgan with her body. Her ears rang from the gunshot, and the acrid odor of gunpowder clogged her nostrils.

Isabelle released the breath she hadn't realized she was holding, then gasped at the onslaught of throbbing, debilitating pain in her shoulder. She clutched at the spot, and warm goo covered her fingers.

It was blood. Her blood.

As they raced toward the address on the GPS app, Jarrod leaned forward in a vain effort to see past the sheets of rain.

Visibility was almost nonexistent despite the high speed of Thomas's windshield wipers. The road they were on was little more than a hard-packed lane transformed into a mud pit. Even though the headlights barely cut through the lashing rain—driven in all directions by the force of the wind—Thomas managed to maneuver around the worst of the puddles.

A black shape appeared on the side of the road.

"That's Morgan's Pontiac," Jarrod said.

"It's the next house on the left." Thomas steered into the cement drive and parked beside another vehicle. "I don't believe it. That's K. C.'s car. What is she doing here?"

"Nothing good," Jarrod muttered.

"What do you mean?"

Jarrod's instincts told him not to wait a second longer. Too much time had already passed since Morgan's interrupted call, but Thomas should know the truth about his wife so he could prepare for whatever they found inside.

"K. C. already knew you were adopted," Jarrod said flatly.

Thomas gaped at him. "I don't believe you."

"Jasper told her."

"How could you possibly know that?" Thomas asked. "Jasper has been unconscious for days."

Jarrod paused to consider what to say. He shouldn't be the one to explain the family relationships. He shrugged as if the answer were obvious. "Morgan told me."

"The woman who told you where to find Isabelle?" Thomas's expression mingled anger with confusion. "Who in the world is this mysterious Morgan? Somehow you keep managing not to tell me."

"Just trust me on this," Jarrod said, his tone grim. "K. C. knew, and she didn't tell you she knew. But right now, we need to focus on what's going on inside those walls. Can I count on you to have my back?"

Thomas glared at him a moment, then nodded. "What do you want me to do?"

"We'll go in that side door. Quietly. Then assess and act."

"I served a tour in the military too, you know."

"I know." *If you hadn't, I'd have left you at the hotel.*

Thomas paused with his hand on the car door handle. "You're positive K. C. already knew?"

"Yes," Jarrod answered. "I'm sorry."

Thomas's face was set in grim lines. "Me too."

Jarrod slid out of the vehicle and pulled his jacket collar around his neck, grateful for even the little protection from the rain provided by the carport roof. The L-shape of the house helped block the worst of the wind. He tried the side door and found it unlocked. Thomas followed close behind him as he entered the kitchen. A fluorescent bulb shone over the sink, giving them enough light to maneuver around the dinette set.

A woman's voice could be heard from the front of the house.

"That's K. C.," Thomas whispered.

Jarrod caught him by the arm as he tried to go past him. "Wait a second."

Streaks of lightning joined with earth-shaking thunder. Shouts reverberated throughout the house.

The sound of a gunshot split the air.

"Isabelle!" Jarrod shouted. "Morgan!"

There was no response.

Jarrod was done with caution. He sprinted around the corner, taking in the scene despite the room being in almost complete darkness. K. C. stood at the other end, tears streaming down her face, holding a revolver that was pointed at the floor. Morgan knelt beside Isabelle, tucking her jacket around her. The front door stood wide open.

"I've got this." Thomas went around Jarrod toward his wife and eased the gun from her grip.

Jarrod knelt down on the other side of Isabelle, noted the wound, and cradled her head in his lap. "Isabelle, can you hear me?"

She shivered and whispered his name. "You're here." Incredibly, the corners of her mouth tilted up in a smile.

The affection in her voice squeezed his heart. He glanced at Thomas, who was already on the phone with 911.

"Help is on the way," Jarrod told her past the lump in his throat. *Please, God, give them wings.* But he knew that the storm would delay the ambulance.

Isabelle stretched her fingers toward him.

He clasped his hand around hers, then pressed his lips against her fingers. "Stay with me, Isabelle."

She nodded and closed her eyes.

As they waited for the ambulance, Thomas perched on the couch with K. C. She alternately sobbed uncontrollably and blamed her campaign manager for everything that had happened.

Morgan retrieved lamps from the other rooms so they were no longer in darkness. She also brought in blankets and a pillow for Isabelle.

After tending to her daughter's comfort, Morgan found a first aid kit in the bathroom. She allowed Jarrod to treat the cuts on her hand where she'd injured herself cutting the ropes around Isabelle's ankles with a shard of glass. While he bandaged the wounds, she told them about Robert's murder-suicide plan and how he'd run out the front door after firing the revolver.

Thomas called Captain Palmer with the news that Robert had assaulted Morgan and shot Isabelle. The captain promised to put out an all-points bulletin to every law enforcement officer on the island and the nearby mainland. Jarrod doubted the man would get away.

Instead of following Robert, K. C. had picked up the gun he'd dropped. Had she intended to carry out the plan? Or had she simply panicked and picked it up without thinking of the consequences?

Jarrod didn't know, and he didn't really care. His sympathies were with Thomas, whose shoulders bowed as if he were burdened with the weight of the world. What did a guy do after learning that his wife had abducted and considered murdering his sister for her political aspirations and greed? How could anyone recover from such a blow?

Morgan watched Thomas as she idly toyed with the diamond ring on her finger. "Does he know who I am?" she asked Jarrod quietly.

"He's a smart guy," Jarrod answered. "I'm sure he's guessed."

"I don't know what to say to him." Her sigh was light as a feather yet layered with heartache.

"I'm not sure you need to *say* anything." Jarrod bit his lower lip against the dull edge of old grief he experienced whenever he thought of his mother. "Sometimes a man just needs to know his mom is beside him."

"You're very wise." Morgan leaned forward and gave him a peck on the cheek. "But if you break Isabelle's heart, I won't be so nice."

"I never will," Jarrod promised.

Despite his concern for Isabelle, he couldn't help smiling as Morgan perched on the couch arm beside Thomas and gently took his hand, murmuring soothingly. Somehow the weight Thomas carried already seemed a little lighter.

Rain pounded against the hospital window, but Isabelle felt safe against the onslaught. Almost as soon as she arrived at the ER, she'd been whisked into surgery. Afterward, the surgeon assured her that she'd been lucky. The bullet was easily removed, and she probably wouldn't have any lasting damage from the wound.

No, she wasn't lucky. She was blessed in more ways than one.

A knock sounded on the door, and Jarrod appeared with a bouquet of flowers in one hand and a cup of chocolate pudding in the other. "Mind if I come in?"

Isabelle's cheeks heated. "Please do."

He stood near her bed, his gaze direct. "I told you before. We've got to stop meeting like this."

"Where would you rather meet?" she teased.

Jarrod chuckled. "How about somewhere without blood and bullets?"

His expression tugged at her heart. It was almost surreal that they were here together, and she couldn't believe how important he'd become to her in a few short days. She hesitated to think about the future—if they even had a future. Perhaps it was enough to simply enjoy the blessing of today. At least for the time being.

He placed the pudding cup on the nightstand and handed her the bouquet. "These are for you. Notice there are no black or purple tulips. Only daisies and yellow roses. Touches of sunshine in the rain."

"How did you know?"

"Know what?" Jarrod bent toward her over the railing.

"That's one of my favorite Florida weather quirks." Isabelle let herself get lost for a moment in his hazel eyes, their golden flecks also bits of sunshine. At least to her. She blushed again. "When the sun shines during a rainstorm."

"It's one of my favorite weather quirks too."

Delighted by the romantic side of Jarrod's nature, Isabelle cradled the bouquet and breathed in the lovely fragrances. Less than a week ago, she'd been frightened by tulip petals and a threatening note. Now here she was reveling in the flowers given to her by the man of her dreams.

Okay, it wasn't going to be that easy not to think about the future. Why did Jarrod have to be so courageous, confident, competent, and compassionate? He was everything she admired in her fictional heroes. Everything she desired in a real flesh-and-blood man.

"Do you think you're up to more company?" Jarrod straightened and glanced toward the door. "A couple of people want to see you."

"Is Morgan here?"

He nodded. "And Thomas."

"I'd love to see them." Another blessing. Even though no one could replace her adoptive parents in her heart, Isabelle was humbly grateful that the secret birth certificates had led her to her birth mom and her brother. She no longer felt so alone.

"I'll tell them to come in," Jarrod said.

Isabelle caught his arm as he turned to go. "First tell me about K. C. and Robert. What happened?"

"Robert was apprehended when he tried to steal a car. Last I heard from Captain Palmer, he and K. C. are blaming each other while proclaiming total innocence." He took her hand. "It's a mess, but they're both headed to prison. They can never harm you again."

"I'm glad, but I'm sorry for Thomas."

"Me too. He knew K. C. was ambitious, but he had no idea the lengths she'd go to get what she wanted." Jarrod paused, then continued. "The police lab compared your bullet with the one they took out of Jasper. They matched."

"You mean K. C. was the woman in the mask?" Of course she was. K. C. had the same slender frame as the shooter. Why hadn't Isabelle noticed the resemblance before? But even if she'd accused K. C. of trying to kill her in Jasper's office, she doubted anyone would have believed her. Why would anyone in this town believe their respected county commissioner was capable of such evil?

"The story is jumbled, but it appears K. C. told Robert that Jasper knew about Thomas's adoption," Jarrod explained. "Robert saw you with Jasper and recognized you from his earlier research into Thomas's background. After K. C. sent the anonymous text to Jasper, Robert broke into the office to find out exactly how much Jasper knew."

"And then she decided to kill us?" An involuntary shiver shook Isabelle's body.

"She says she only meant to scare you both," he answered. "But Jasper must have realized it was her. That's why he said her name."

She squeezed his hand. "How is Jasper?"

"He regained consciousness this morning." Jarrod ran his hand down his face. "And he's a little cranky that he missed out on all the action. A full recovery is going to take some time. But every day is a step forward. He wants to see you. To apologize."

"Apologize for what? This wasn't his fault."

"He thinks it is." Jarrod blew out a long breath. "He told me that he went to the realty office to talk to Thomas, but K. C. was there. He made the mistake of telling her about Thomas's adoption."

"She already knew."

"But that conversation told her that Jasper knew. And K. C. didn't want him telling you or Thomas. At least not until after the election. Jasper blames himself for everything that happened."

"He saved my life and helped me find my family." Isabelle sank deeper into the pillows propped behind her and winced at the ache in her shoulder. "Everything is going to be fine. I know it."

Isabelle wasn't sure where that certainty came from. Maybe from that same place as the peace she'd felt earlier when Robert had spoken so cavalierly of her death and Morgan demonstrated such deep tranquility.

A peace truly beyond understanding.

Jarrod ushered Morgan and Thomas into the room.

After the initial greetings and assurances from Isabelle that she was sore but fine, Morgan sighed. "I've been so worried I could hardly breathe."

"How did you know where to find me?" Isabelle asked.

"I was coming to the hotel to see you and tell you everything," Morgan explained. "When I pulled into the parking garage, K. C. was leaving. You were in the back seat with that horrid man, your head propped against the window. I knew something was wrong, so I followed them."

"I'm glad you did," Isabelle said.

"Me too."

"And me," Thomas added.

An awkward silence followed.

Jarrod cleared his throat. "I should put those flowers in water."

"Yes, please." Isabelle handed the bouquet to him.

"They're lovely," Morgan remarked.

"Thank you," Isabelle and Jarrod chorused at the same time.

Everyone laughed. Then the uncomfortable silence returned.

Jarrod turned his back on the group as he filled a pitcher with water. All the pent-up emotion in the room was getting to him. There was so much that needed to be said.

He glanced at Morgan. Her usually placid expression seemed troubled by regret and lost chances. She nervously twisted her ring around her finger—the ring with the corded band set with a diamond and two blue stones. Could they be . . . ?

Jarrod placed the pitcher, now adorned with the bouquet, on Isabelle's nightstand. "That's an interesting ring you're wearing, Morgan. Very unique."

A small smile lifted the corners of her mouth. She fiddled with it, then removed it from her finger and handed it to Isabelle. "Davis gave me this ring when he helped me with my new identity."

"These are our birthstones." Isabelle handed the ring to Thomas. "Blue zircon."

"I'm guessing the diamond is for you," Thomas said as he examined the ring. "Your birthday's in April?"

"Morgan's birth date is in August," Morgan said. "But yes, I was born on April 10. Davis wanted me to have something to connect me with who I truly was. And with my two darling babies." Her eyes glistened with tears. "At the time I didn't think he understood how much I hated myself, that I didn't want to connect to the old me anymore. But he knew me better than I knew myself, and he insisted that someday I would be glad I had this ring. He was right. I rarely take it off. Not a day has passed when I haven't thought of you both."

Thomas drew Morgan into a hug as her tears flowed, and then he grasped Isabelle's hand.

Jarrod backed out of the room as the little family, now restored, wept tears of sorrow for their lost time and joy for the promise of a united future.

The rain beat a steady rhythm against the hospital windowpanes the next day. The tropical storm had veered up the coast and out to sea, leaving behind torn roof shingles, broken tree limbs, and flooding in the island's low spots. The island residents had been spared the devastation of a full-blown hurricane.

Isabelle stood at the window, gazing out into the darkness and contemplating the storm that had disrupted her own peaceful existence over the past week. Neither she nor Thomas had asked Morgan about their biological fathers or why she'd started down such a destructive path as a young teen. Isabelle sensed that Michelle's relationship with her dad was nothing like Isabelle's had been with the same man. Had her grandfather changed so much that he drove his daughter away, yet managed to develop a loving, close relationship with Isabelle?

Perhaps some questions were better left in the past.

They did learn that Isabelle's grandfather had known about Michelle's first pregnancy and wanted nothing to do with the baby. Davis selected the Reids as Thomas's parents without his father's knowledge. Davis and his wife adopted Isabelle because, by that time, they'd discovered they could have no children of their own. The Byrnes left the state with Michelle for several months and returned with their newborn infant. Not even their closest friends knew of Isabelle's true parentage. Though she had no proof, Isabelle wanted to believe her grandfather knew the truth of her parentage. Maybe he doted on her to make up for how he'd treated his daughter.

In the window's reflection, Isabelle saw her door open. She spun around and smiled at Jarrod.

"Is it too late for me to stop by?" he asked.

"Not at all. I'm glad you're here."

Jarrod joined her at the window. "How was your visit with Thomas and Morgan last night?"

"Wonderful. And sad and happy." She peered up at him. "You didn't have to leave."

"I think I did." He leaned against the windowsill. "Besides, I needed to take care of a little matter regarding your wicked stepmother."

"Heather?" Isabelle shook her head. "I'm not upset that she didn't come to see me. Can you imagine what it's going to be like introducing her to Morgan?"

"It was something more serious than that." Jarrod dug into his pocket and pulled out a few black tulip petals. "She's the one who tried to scare you away."

Isabelle opened her mouth to protest, then shut it again. After she'd accused K. C. of leaving the notes, she'd realized that whoever had actually done it must have known about the birth certificates. Heather and Reuben were in on that secret. Heather had known where Isabelle planned to stay. And yet . . .

"How did she do it?" Isabelle asked. "She was still at home when I arrived at the cottage."

"That's what she wanted you to think. But Samantha did some digging. Heather arrived at the cottage before you did. She made you think she was still at home, but she's been here the entire time. She also took your briefcase and laptop. Samantha found them in a closet in your hotel suite."

Isabelle still found it hard to believe. Except it was easy to believe. Childish and ominous all rolled up into one scary threat. So like Heather.

"She's also the one who tampered with your brakes," Jarrod continued. "Captain Palmer has a warrant out for her arrest."

Her stomach dropped. "You mean K. C. She tampered with the brakes."

"No, Heather did it," he said. "And now she's gone."

Isabelle lowered herself to a chair. Her heart refused to accept what Jarrod was saying. "Why would she do that?"

Jarrod bent beside her and took her hands in his. "My guess is that she wanted control over your family's fortune. And after everything she went through to get it, she'll probably end up forfeiting even what she would have inherited if she'd been happy with her rightful share. I'm sorry she's like that."

"So am I," Isabelle said. She gently pulled her hands away, then ran her fingers along his jawline. In this moment, she wanted to shove all thoughts of K. C. and Heather aside—to forget, at least for a little while, all the trouble and hurt they'd caused because of their greed. Instead, she wanted to lose herself in the depth of Jarrod's caring gaze and never leave. Except she needed to know the answer to one more important question. "Who's Samantha?" *Do you have a girlfriend—or worse, a wife? Have I been unwittingly threatening a marriage?*

But Jarrod's grin eased her mind at once. "One of my security officers. She tailed you from the hotel to the clinic when you met Thomas. Robert noticed her as she followed you back to the hotel, and he got the jump on her in the parking garage when you were kidnapped."

"Is she all right?"

"She's fine. Since she solved the mystery of the tulips and the brakes, I plan to keep her around. Maybe give her a promotion."

Isabelle didn't want to talk about Samantha anymore. Or Heather or black tulips or brakes. She stared out the window and traced a raindrop on the cold glass.

Jarrod shifted, angling his body toward hers. "Now that all the mysteries have been solved, I guess you'll be going home soon."

Had she imagined the wistfulness in his voice, or was he truly sad that she might leave? She prayed the latter, but there was only one way to find out.

"Morgan and Thomas have asked me to stay here for a while, so we can all spend time together, get to know one another." Isabelle searched his eyes, hoping beyond hope that he wanted that too.

"What did you say?" His voice sounded husky.

"I said yes."

Jarrod gently pulled her into his arms, then smiled as he lowered his mouth to hers.

Isabelle kissed him back and lost herself in dreams of adding Jarrod's name to her family tree.

Up to this point, we've been doing all the writing. Now it's *your* turn!

Tell us what you think about this book, the characters, the bad guy, or anything else you'd like to share with us about this series. We can't wait to hear from *you*!

Log on to give us your feedback at:
https://www.surveymonkey.com/r/sweetintrigue

Annie's® FICTION